The Purple Lotus

AND OTHER STORIES

The Purple Lotus

AND OTHER STORIES

Ratna Rao Shekar

*Mapin*Lit

An Imprint of Mapin Publishing

First published in India in 2011 by
Mapin Publishing Pvt Ltd
502 Paritosh, Near Darpana Academy,
Usmanpura Riverside,
Ahmedabad 380013
T: 91 79 4022 8228
F: 91 79 4022 8201
E: mapin@mapinpub.com
www.mapinpub.com

Simultaneously published in the
United States of America in 2011 by
Grantha Corporation
77 Daniele Drive, Hidden Meadows
Ocean Township, NJ 07712
E: mapin@mapinpub.com

Distributors
North America:
Antique Collectors' Club
T: 1 800 252 5231
E: info@antiquecc.com
www.antiquecollectorsclub.com

Southeast Asia:
Paragon Asia Co. Ltd
T: 66 2877 7755 • F: 66 2468 9636
E: info@paragonasia.com

Australia & New Zealand:
Peribo Pty Ltd
T: 61 2 9457 0011
E: michael.coffey@peribo.com.au

Austria, Germany, The Netherlands
and Switzerland:
Visual Books Sales Agency
T: 49 30 69 819 007
F: 49 30 69 819 005
E: service@visualbooks-sales.com

UK and Europe (excluding Austria,
Germany,
The Netherlands and Switzerland):
Gazelle Book Service Ltd
T: 44 1524 68765 • F: 44 1524 63232
E: sales@gazellebooks.co.uk

Rest of the world:
Mapin Publishing Pvt Ltd

This book is a work of fiction. Names, characters, places and incidents are used fictitiously. Any resemblance to actual events, locales or persons, living or dead is entirely coincidental.

ISBN: 978-81-89995-59-1 (Mapin)
ISBN: 978-1-935677-17-8 (Grantha)
LCCN: 2011935724

Cover and book design by
Gitanjali Mehta Anand

Typeset in Berkeley Oldstyle

Printed in India at Pragati Offset Pvt. Ltd.
Hyderabad
www.pragati.com

The paper used in this publication meets the minimum requirements of the American National Standards for Permanence of Paper for Printed Library Materials.

For Minakshi
and Kartikeya

For who they have grown up to be

CONTENTS

9 The American in Banaras

21 The Purple Lotus

29 Ahalya's Anguish

37 Road No.3, Banjara Hills

44 Amethyst

47 Talk to Me

57 A Piece of My Heart

66 The Mona Lisa Smile

81 A Character in Search of a Writer

92 Boa Mama, Who Will Sing Your Songs?

95 One of a Kind

105 We Were Young Once

113 My Name is Meenakshi

THE AMERICAN IN BANARAS

HOW DID HE, David, imagine that he could live away from the sounds and smells of Banaras, he asked himself as he walked from the two-bedroomed house that he had rented for a few months near the Banaras Hindu University. Stopping for a *jalebi* and hot milk in a narrow and crowded *gully*, he thought, and ah, where else could he hope to discuss local politics with others who came for their milk served in a *kulhad*, hot and steaming, though most of them seemed to be sitting around only because they had nothing else to do, and occasionally participated in the ongoing discussion with some comment.

The *seth*, a burly, moustachioed fellow, wearing nothing but a *banian* and *dhoti* like a true *Banarasi*, sat boiling and stirring the milk as if the present moment was all, much like a Zen monk meditating on what might seem to others routine, but to him defined his life and its purpose.

In the years David had been away for almost a decade to the day last month – he had lost touch with local gossip and politics but not his umbilical connection with this city, the ancient city of Kashi as he liked to think of it, the city that might have been in existence before creation itself. This was the city he had first come to as a young student of Sanskrit in search of a teacher, whom he had found in Dr Ganapathi Mishra.

"Sir, this country will be having its general elections once again in a month. We don't want to go to vote, everyone is a rascal. We don't even have electricity or water on a normal day, why should we make the effort to go to polling booths?" someone sitting next to him said.

David thought the man was talking to someone else until he realized the remark was directed to him. The man gently pulled the sleeve of David's blue *khadi kurta* to get his attention. "Where are you from sir? The United States presumably. Now we want leaders like your Obama," he said beginning to confide in David as if he were a friend of many years. David knew the next thing this man would ask him was if he had any children. 'Issues' they called them, and certainly his daughter was an issue, wanting a fancy car so that she could start graduate school at Penn.

It was a hot, humid day and David wiped his face with a red *gamchha*, a multipurpose piece of cloth that he could use for wiping his face or his body when he bathed in the Ganga. The cloth could further morph into a bag to carry vegetables. These guys knew a thing or two about recycling, so there Al Gore, he said to himself commending the genius of the *Banarasi*.

His face had begun to turn red from the heat, but there was nothing else he wanted to do this moment than be in Kashi, amongst these simple men, he thought smiling to himself. The man next to him thought he was smiling at something he had said and felt compelled to draw himself up to launch into a harangue on the politics of the state or of the state of Banaras itself.

"*Bhayyaji*, have one more hot *jalebi*, please," the *seth* said showing the kind of affection that even his mother in Connecticut did not express. "No thank you, not one more, I really can't," he said pulling back his small palm-leaf *katori* to where the *seth*'s large arm or the large steel slotted serving spoon that drained out the hot oil could not reach. But who listens to anyone in India? Things moved on their own volition not unlike the wheels of the Juggernaut that he and his guru would often sit talking about.

And before he knew it, there was another syrupy, hot, orange *jalebi* in his *katori*. Kate would have asked if this was a 'permitted' colour but he was not going to worry about all that, considering she was not with him. Quite unlikely that she would ever be with him again given that they were on the verge of a divorce he thought, mentally tapping himself on his own shoulder.

He wanted to tell these rambunctious, if good-hearted men around him that he was getting divorced, and that he had no wife for the moment. Everyone here asked how many children but never ever asked if you had a wife. That you had a 'Mrs' was understood, even expected. They even addressed the Mrs, not just his but anyone's, respectfully either as '*bhabhi*' or '*didi*'.

He wanted to tell them that though he loved his daughter Surya, he had never been so relieved in his life than when Kate had announced that she wanted a divorce. She never understood the Indian part of him, his Hinduism, his yoga or his love for Banaras. Once, when they were a little more in love than in the past few years, he had suggested she come with him to Banaras. She had accused him of thoughtlessly wanting to expose her to diseases and pestilence that she imagined were rampant in India. She never did come to India with him, not even up to Lutyens' Delhi that was such a befitting capital of the British Empire.

He had hoped Surya would come with him this time for he had so wanted to show her all that he loved about the country, its friendly and garrulous people, its gods who had temples even on busy street junctions, and the chaos... But, he shook his head doubtfully for although she had told him initially she wanted to take Sanskrit classes in freshman year, she changed her mind soon enough to opt for Spanish. She too showed no love for a country that was dear to him above all else.

Why had he married her mother in the first place, these gentlemen around him might want to know. He smiled genially at another man sitting to his left, wanting to tell him the story of his life. People here had so much friendship and warmth in their hearts that no one would think it unusual if he did launch into the story of his marriage. This was so unlike how it would be like back home in Harvard where he was a professor of theology and world religions. He was certainly glad he was among these warm strangers in Banaras, far from the ruthless Boston winters.

All of a sudden, everyone was lulled into a moment of silence and respect as they saw another dead body being carried to the *ghats* by anxious relatives and friends who wanted to cremate the body before sundown.

He remembered how shocked he had been initially when he came here as a 23-year-old to see the casualness with which the dead were treated in Banaras. They might as well have been carrying the day's groceries the way they hauled a body on their shoulders and walked towards the *ghats*. "*Ram naam satya hai*", the men chanted sonorously as they took the body covered with a white sheet and decked with flowers towards Harishchandra Ghat where the guards or *doms* as they were called, were among the richest men in the city. Or so it was rumoured.

Even before the pallbearers disappeared into the winding lane, as in the theatre of the absurd, his newfound friends began to get back to their business. The *seth* to the stirring of the milk and the making of another batch of *jalebis*, a few people to the day's business, while others, he was sure, would go for a round of *kushti* or a ritual massage. This was the *mauj masti* of Kashi, the celebration of living. Death was accepted fact in Banaras, and what had to be done with grace was the business of living, David thought to himself as he got up to go to the *ghats* before dusk fell.

"Thank you, *bhayyaji*. Please come tomorrow evening if you are free, all these good men will be here again," said the *seth* accepting the loose change David was giving him. "Never mind, sir. You can always pay me tomorrow," he said with genuine warmth when he saw David fumbling for the rupee coins. There was such faith in human beings in this country, David thought in amazement, and no one worried what would happen to their business even if death called a customer away the next day. Life was not all commerce and he was sure the *seth* had waived many loans in such contingencies, many a time.

But life certainly was about alimonies and settlements in the country of his birth, he mused sadly. He was sure Kate was going to ask for a huge alimony even if she herself taught in an art school, and had a rich father who he had never liked, but who was what was considered old money in Boston. He could not afford the alimony but if it set him free of a marriage he was not sure he could tolerate any longer, he would gladly pay what he was asked.

Well, that would give him the freedom to breathe the air of Banaras once again, even if his guru had since passed away. He had been a gentle soul who had treated him like a son, more than a son in fact, since his own sons had wanted to become engineers and IT professionals. He had taught him all that he had to teach from the intricacies of yoga to Tantric Hinduism.

He had initiated him into a tradition of Hinduism that few cared to understand. A smile of love came upon David's face as he thought of the man who had been more than a father to him, and his wife, the gentle lady he called Ma, who would ply him with rich Banarasi food and fatten him up and urge him to marry soon so that he could become a householder and not remain a *brahmachari* forever. He certainly missed them.

But at that time he had been still too raw inside from his encounter with Nandita to think of marriage. How did they meet, this Indian lady and the yogi, his friends at the *jalebi* shop might have asked, and he would have become as loquacious as them when telling the story. Even in fiction such a story might have seemed impossible, with the novelist having to justify his characters meeting in another appropriate setting. But life itself was full of coincidences and the unexpected his guru would have told him.

He had met her on a flight from New York to Delhi. The most unlikely of places to meet the woman who was to be the love of his life, but where else could he have met her except in a world that was neither hers nor his, but in the vast skies on an aeroplane?

They had been sitting next to each other and had not exchanged anything beyond a smile, when the plane began to go through a thunderstorm and an announcement came over the system that they would be returning to JFK. She had seemed so young and scared that he had held her hand, comforting her with a prayer.

"What was that prayer you were saying?" she had later asked him, beginning to talk to him when the plane had taken off again.

"A *mantra* to protect us. I have a special one for when planes are about to crash and young women are on the verge of a breakdown. And now what could your name be? Nandita, is it?"

"My god, how could you know that!" she had asked, prising her seat belt off to turn towards him.

"I was behind you at the check-in counter and almost all of your boxes and hand luggage had your name on them," he had said, smiling at her naivety.

"Oh, how silly of me to think you have magical or divine powers," she had said turning away, almost disappointed. And yes, he knew from her suitcases that she was married.

"So what were you doing in America?" he had asked her. "Visiting relatives?" Indian women, especially married ones, did not travel alone and here she was without that lucky man who was her husband.

"Why do your assumptions have to be so predictable? I was trying to finish my Ph.D.," Nandita had said. "At Chicago. Northwestern." He had not asked her of course but that he thought she would be doing something so clichéd as visiting her extended family stung her to the core.

He saw her notice that he was a vegetarian, almost spartan in his ways of eating. He had said he got up at 4 am in his guru's house to do the ritual *puja* for Shiva and Devi, his consort. Not only that, he knew all there was to know about yoga, in practice and precept, and the sacred treatises in Sanskrit and Hindi. He told her he loved to read Kalidasa in Sanskrit for diversion, even in bed before he turned off the lights. His favourite? *Kumarasambhava*, a copy of which he gave her on the flight, inscribing it in pencil lightly 'to Nandita, a friend of many lives'.

"I used to play music, you know, Bob Dylan and the like. Write my own songs too. But then Shiva beckoned me to Banaras. And Devi took me to my guru," he had told her.

"But why did you want to study Sanskrit, David?" she had asked him, puzzled.

"I know it's a dead language, and there is nothing much I can do with it but teach at Harvard," he had said, smiling in amusement. He noticed that she was looking into his blue eyes, but had turned away embarrassed when she realized he had seen her interest. He also realized that that she was still holding his hand though there was nothing turbulent about the weather now and the plane was cruising along quite smoothly.

At Heathrow, they got off, had coffee, and walked around the airport holding hands.

"You know Nandita, I have a bit of Scottish blood in me, though I don't much care for the British," he had said breaking into a song in brogue she could not understand but which made her laugh. "I am also quarter Italian from my mother's side. Much like the *khichdi* you guys like to eat."

At another time he had said rather shyly, "May I say something, Nandita? I think you are such an elegant woman; I like the way you wear those Indian clothes. And your husband? What shall I say, except that he is a lucky man."

"Thank you, David. I do hope you will come and visit us in Madras one day. And maybe meet your favourite people – a few more Sanskrit gurus. Madras University has some erudite scholars. Maybe Naren and I could drive you to Chidambaram. You know, the Nataraja temple is one of my favourite temples in all of south India. It's so breathtaking."

"If Chidambaram is your favourite temple, I would like to go with you, Nandita," he had said wistfully. "Though in Banaras too we have a manifestation of the Shiva."

He had looked from across the table where they were having coffee in the cafeteria and said, "You know, Nandita, that *sardarji* there is looking at us and thinking what a fine couple we make. He thinks I am taking my wife of two years to visit her parents in Madras," David said, putting his hand on hers as she gently tried to pull it away.

"David, how does he know we are going to Delhi?" she had asked trying not to look in the direction of the *sardar*.

"Do you have to be so practical and ask me so many questions? C'mon now, they've announced the flight to Delhi. We must be going," David had said pulling her up to her feet, and slinging on his backpack. She paid for the coffee.

And David didn't refuse, as he never had too much money on him. American students like him never had any, even if they were from Harvard and topped their class. "Harvard? They just let me teach undergrads for peanuts. Bonded labour, I call it. And do you think these undergrads are interested in anything I say on Buddhism or Hinduism? They are sitting in my class to fulfill a course requirement," he had grumbled.

When she went to sit by the window along with David she found that the *sardarji* was sitting by them in the aisle. His name was Gurcharan, David whispered to her, after he had introduced himself. While David was busy talking to him, Nandita had slept on his shoulder, and he held her as if she were a young girl.

David realized that such easy intimacy didn't come easy to an Indian woman. But when she had opened her eyes to ask David if it was alright to fall in love even if you were married, he smiled, patted her face and said, "Don't worry love, just sleep. You will feel nice and fresh when this plane lands in Delhi, but before that, this kind hostess will keep waking you up several times for breakfast and lunch and juices... I have never figured why they give you so much to eat on Air India."

He had seen many beautiful faces, but there was something breathtaking about this almost Audrey Hepburn-like face with high cheekbones, a face that was now lying, eyes closed, in his lap.

He had felt a momentary hunger. Of wanting to take her with him. But in India, marriage was sacred. Though he had never met Naren, he had thought of him as a brother of many lives gone by. He would take good care of this woman with whom he felt an inexplicable connection. In Tantric Buddhism they believed that good friends and those you love will meet each other in every birth until salvation. Well, he was prepared to postpone even nirvana if it meant having her as his wife for one lifetime at least.

Despite the philosophy he read, and despite the rigours and discipline of his studies, the farewell at Delhi had been difficult. She had had tears in her eyes when he let her step out of the plane first. In that instant he knew his soul had left his body and would now forever hover around her, wanting to look at her every moment of its existence.

Nandita, she of the high cheekbones. He smiled to himself and wondered what she might be doing right now at this very moment. They had written to each other desultorily, she had even sent him a picture of her daughter Soundarya, immediately after she was born. For a long time he had had that picture of Nandita and her daughter on his desk in his office at the university.

He subsequently married Kate, a friend he had grown up with in Connecticut. When Surya was born, there was peace for a while in the marriage. He was not sure why he had got married in such desperation. Maybe because he didn't want people to think he was different, even queer.

Besides, his guru too had urged him to get married and settle down. He was not sure he would ever find an Indian bride. He was too American in his ways for that. And he was too much of a Hindu for an American to accept him. But Kate did, or he had imagined for a few years that he had found a woman who could accept that part of him: his love for tradition, reading Sanskrit texts and his yogic practices.

In recent years, he had received only one letter from Nandita, written in that beautiful hand of hers. She wrote to tell him that her daughter Soundarya was going to be married soon, and that she and Naren wanted him to come for the wedding in Madras. "It would make me so happy to see you again, David," she had written in the letter that she sent along with the invitation. How quickly our children grow up, he wanted to tell Nandita, putting the invitation away with a sense of longing.

Soundarya was a graduate in aeronautical engineering. She obviously did not share her mother's love for literature. He remembered that in the few hours that he had spent with Nandita at the airport they had read through her Graham Greene. He wondered if she would remember that.

If he was going to be 53, how old would she be? She was about the same age he was, she had told him later when he had gone to meet her and Naren in Madras. Would she be the same Nandita who had slept on his shoulder on the flight almost 30 years ago?

Life and its everyday struggles would have changed her, as it had him. They were different people now, so many decades later, but who knows if some things still remained the same within them and between them? He was then the young, callow youth who was coming to India to seek a meaning to his life, and she, a young woman who had chosen marriage far too early.

David hurried to the *ghats*. He wanted to be there before the evening *aarti* was performed for the Ganga, a river so integral to the lives of Indians that it was considered sacred. He wished they would not make such a song and dance about these things to attract tourists. He did not remember any of this pageantry three decades ago when he had first come to Banaras. But things had changed even in this city where time, he often imagined, sat lightly.

Tomorrow he would take a flight to Delhi and from there make the train journey to Madras. Even the name of the city had changed. To Chennai. If he could persuade Nandita, he would like to go with her to Chidambaram to see the Nataraja temple, where Shiva, the ascetic appears as the ecstatic dancer, setting the world into motion. Yet, how could he forget that the god here concealed as much as he revealed?

He didn't know what life held for him beyond this day, he thought, as he watched the sun set over the Ganga. He dipped his head into the water and, standing waist deep in it, looked, not at the sun setting on another day, but within him. Into that silence, deep within where he hoped to find some understanding.

THE PURPLE LOTUS

THE LOTUS, FRANGIPANI and incense fragrances of the dark caverns had been part of Bhikkhu Ananda ever since he stepped into the Dambulla monastery. All that he could remember of that wet day when he had to leave home to go to the monastery was his mother weeping unabashedly; in fact like nothing he had seen before, when his father lifted him into the bus. She and his little sister had stood by the winding mountain road waving to him until he could not see them any longer. It would be an eight-hour journey his father had told him, peeling a banana, asking him to eat to keep hunger away.

He, however, didn't want to eat, but only cry and ask his father why he was being taken away from home. Why me, he mumbled to himself softly as he fell asleep on the bus, beside his father.

He was only a child, and no one had told him about the long tradition of one child from every family being dedicated to a monastery so that Buddhism might survive in the country. This is how it was in Sri Lanka, to which Sanghamitta and Mahendra, children of King Asoka, had brought not only a branch of the Bo tree from Bodh Gaya, but also the Enlightened One's teachings.

"Prostrate before *Guruthuma* Sambhava," his father commanded when they arrived at the monastery. Young Ananda unhesitatingly fell at the feet of the *Guruthuma*, who raised his hand in blessing without a trace of emotion.

On the first evening itself they peeled his clothes away to give him the yellow robe of the initiate. He did not mind that they took the lovely new shirt that his mother had bought him for his birthday – the green shirt that made him a hero among his friends who played cricket with him in the narrow streets of the town. What he did mind was that the next morning his dark-brown silky hair was sheared off so that when he ran his small hands on his head he found he was bald. There were no mirrors in the monastery, only the sympathetic smile of Lusantha, another initiate, no older than his own eight years.

And during those early morning hours when he wanted to snuggle into the blanket imagining he was by the side of his mother who often drew him to her at this time of the night, he heard the repeated sound of the gong in the *vihara*. His friend shook him awake.

"But it's only three in the morning!" he cried to Lusantha who said he must now wake up, as they had to have a bath and go the central hall for food.

Ananda was not even hungry at that early hour, but when Lusantha remarked that there would be no other meal until four in the evening, he woke up to get ready and go to the dining hall with the steel *paththaraya* that he had been given the previous morning, by a fellow monk.

A senior student came with hot tea that was poured into the *paththaraya* and even as he was trying to drink it without scalding his tongue, two pieces of bread were thrust into his hands. He ate greedily and waited for more.

"What are you waiting for, friend? That is all we will get this morning. Let's hurry for prayer before some senior *bhikkhu* berates us," Lusantha said, standing behind him.

That life was going to be hard, he realized when he opened his books. What he had to learn at the school in his hometown was easier than what he was asked to learn at this monastery: Buddhist texts, in both Sanskrit and Pali, Sinhalese literature and history, and worse, astronomy and mathematics. He wished for a miracle that would make his father change his heart, and come and fetch him.

But it did not look as if *Guruthuma* Sambhava would let him go home even if the miracle occurred – did this man ever smile, he now speculated, and in all the ten years he had been here, he hardly saw *Guruthuma* smile – and he knew life wasn't going to give him much choice, and decided to immerse himself in the Pali and Sanskrit texts.

As he began getting used to life in the monastery, what he liked most was going to the caves to look at the Buddha figures painted on the walls and ceilings, and those that were sculpted out; and, those incense and lotus smells of the caves that he soon began to associate with his austere life as a monk initiate.

"Lusantha, why are there so many Buddhas, all in one cave?" he had asked Lusantha one morning, unable to solve the mystery of over 25 Buddhas in one dark cave.

"Maybe the sculptors decided they wanted the best possible Buddha figure, and having made them didn't want to destroy them. I know some Buddhas don't have their noses right or some, the ears. Who knows? If only *Guruthuma* Sambhava would talk more, we could ask him," said Lusantha.

They concluded that maybe the Sinhala kings wanted to show how devout they were by commissioning and paying for many Buddha figures. Whatever their conjectures, they placed lamps before each of the Buddhas, as commanded by a senior monk.

Ananda often sought solace in the warmth of the Dambulla Caves, amongst these benevolent Buddhas. He liked all the Buddhas in their bright colours of yellow, green and orange, and some with additional gold paint. But best of all he liked the reclining figure of the Shakyamuni in the *Parinirvana* posture.

Here the Shakyamuni was spread across a whole cave, with the head at one end, and feet with red *chakra*s painted on the soles at the other, eyes almost closed as this was the moment when he would extinguish his physical body and attain *nirvana*. Ananda liked bringing offerings of flowers and pineapples, rice and cups of tea to the Buddhas in the early hours of the morning.

During moments such as these, in the hush of the cave that was at least a few centuries old, he became calm. He even forgot his mother's hands on his head, oh yes, a head that was now bald. Enlightenment and liberation for that matter even the continuation of the long tradition of Theravada Buddhism, were unknown to him – he, who was growing into a handsome young man despite, or primarily because of, the austere life he was leading.

He read the *Dhammapada* in Pali, a language in which he had become quite fluent. He knew by memory many strictures from the 423 verses of this early Buddhist text. But however much he read the strictures about capturing the monkey-mind, it seemed that even after hours of sitting still in meditation he could not achieve any sense of balance.

He recited aloud that morning... "And one recites a hundred verses/ With words of no avail, better is one *Dhamma* word/ having heard which one is pacified". Who would give him that one *Dhamma* word that would still his wavering mind? When would that moment come when he would know what his path in life would be?

Recently, he had been watching a young girl coming to the temples in the monastery, usually in the evenings, with two purple lotuses that she placed before the Buddha, in what was believed to be the oldest cave in the monastery. She wore the traditional dress of Sinhalese girls, the *Lama Sariya*, a long white skirt with a frilled blouse. She had dark, dazzling eyes that seemed to have a life of their own, independent of the person she was.

Ananda saw her climbing the steep stairs, always briskly, going into one temple after another, lighting an incense stick or sometimes placing a pineapple or bananas before the multiple Buddhas, but keeping her two purple lotuses for the Buddha in the oldest cave.

As an initiate he had taken the vows of celibacy but he could not help looking out for her arrival in the evenings, when he would sit in silence by himself in the verandah. And one evening while going past him, she raised her eyes to look at him. He imagined she even smiled at him.

He had looked away hurriedly, got up from where he was sitting, and had gone looking for Lusantha. Had his friend ever fallen in love? How could you fall in love with someone you did not even speak with?

And for the first time he understood how difficult it must have been for young Siddhartha to leave behind his young wife and a newborn son, to seek answers to the death and sorrow that he saw all around him outside the palace, where he had lived cocooned from the realities of life.

One day, when she came with her mother, he heard her calling out to the girl, "Anjalika, can you not run up like that? You know I am old, I cannot take the stairs like you do so quickly."

Anjalika, so that was her name. He watched her pause just a little so that her mother could catch up with her, but she was a girl in a hurry.

That day, when she raised her eyes to look at him, he was sure she had smiled at him. But why would she smile at a monk in yellow robes and who had nothing that he could call his own? The only thing he possessed was a steel *paththaraya*. What did he have that he could offer her who seemed like a well-to-do girl?

Anjalika sighed, wondering if her mother had seen her smiling at the young monk. But she felt happy here. She liked these caves, and their smells of prayer and benevolence that rose into the evening along with the murmur of chants. She was a pious girl who had grown up in the village near Dambulla. It was her practice to visit the temple in the evenings, whenever she could find time from school and housework.

And now this young *bhikkhu* raised his eyes from the books he was reading, to look at her. She wanted to ask him what his name was, who his parents were, and did he not miss his mother? But girls like her did not speak to young men, even if they were monks. So she could do nothing but meet his glances, even if it were shyly.

On the few evenings when she did not see him sitting on the verandah of the temple, she looked around for him, wondering if he had taken ill or had just gone begging into the town.

He was handsome, no doubt of that. She wondered why of all the boys she knew she was drawn to this young *sadhu*. Had they been connected in a previous life in the wheel of *samsara*? She did not even know his name.

But, she thought to herself, one day this young initiate would become a full-fledged monk and would immerse himself in the duties of the monastery and forget all about her. What use, then, would he have for a girl like her, who liked to wear colourful clothes and beautiful jewellery, sing songs and play with children?

Already her mother had been talking of getting her married to a young man from Colombo which was a big city, she had heard. There would be magnificent temples even there, her mother had told her, but would anything compare with these ancient, warm cave temples?

As the day of his initiation approached, when it would be customary for Ananda to live as a householder for a day, before the senior monks accepted him into one of their community, he began to have moments of self doubt.

Was the path he was taking the right one? If it was, would he ever be able to see Anjalika again? Anjalika and her purple lotus flowers. Just that thought brought up the centuries of sorrow contained within him.

The Enlightened One had said that in attachment was sorrow, but did not attachment also bring with it happiness? To be able to hold Anjalika in his arms. How could that be sorrow? Indeed, the moment when he had to make the choice between the lay life and that of the monk was a difficult one. He began to chant from the *Dhammapada* once again:

"Good is restraint in body,
restraint in speech is good,
good is restraint in mind,
everywhere restraint is good;
the *bhikkhu* everywhere restrained
is from all *dukkha* free."

He hurried into the inner sanctum to join the other *bhikkhus*. "*Buddham Saranam Gacchami, Dhammam Saranam Gacchami, Sangham Charanam Gacchami*. (I seek refuge in the Buddha, I seek refuge in the *Dhamma*, I seek refuge in the Sangha)," he muttered, lost in meditation.

And Anjalika, who continued to come to the Dambulla Caves missed seeing the young monk evening after evening and began to grow sad, though not a word had passed between them.

One day, she brought with her three purple lotuses. She placed two before the Buddha, and the third one, after some hesitation, before the Buddha too.

This was her last visit to the Caves.

AHALYA'S ANGUISH

AHALYA TOOK A deep breath. She tried to settle down comfortably on the grass mat in a room dimly lit by a flickering oil lamp. The traditional make-up of her face alone would take at least three hours. She tried to find a position that would let her lie still while Kannappachettan worked on her face as if it were a canvas.

It was afternoon, but it was dark outside with just a promise of the monsoons. People everywhere waited anxiously for first rains here in Kerala which would then sweep across the country lashing streets, drenching houses and filling streams. She couldn't smell the rain as yet but the temperatures had dropped and the countryside had cooled down. Her '*appa*', who was not her father but her guru, would not allow even fans in classrooms as he felt these would disturb his students' concentration. So they rehearsed or studied in the humidity of the Kerala summer.

This was a small village near Guruvayoor in Kerala. Her *amma* had told her that when she was born, her first outing from her home was to the Krishna temple in Guruvayoor, and they weighed bananas equal to her weight to give the deity. "Only four-and-a-half bananas, not even half a dozen, for this little one who was a gift from Guruvayoorappa himself," her mother had said fondly, stroking the child's hair. She had been lightweight when she was born, they said, and even now her mother saw to it that the elfin-looking Ahalya ate well so that she could withstand the long hours of practice and study that Koodiyattam entailed. She was small-built, and tiny like the four-feet nothing Krishna idol of Guruvayoor whom she now visited often.

She was sent to a convent school in Kodaikanal, where she read Shakespeare, Jane Austen, Charlotte Bronte and Charles Dickens and developed a love for English literature. She so loved Bronte's *Wuthering Heights*, but what she could reread even now, if only she had the leisure, were all of Austen's writings. Austen had lived in such a stifling time, when women were not even taken seriously. Living in Kerala where life could get claustrophobic with tradition, she thought her life was no different from that of a Jane Austen heroine.

She wrote poems and was creative in class, securing excellent grades in English. Her one failing were the sciences – biology and physics – but even that was alright, as she had managed to scrape through her Class 12 exams and topped her school in English. Her friends were applying to go to colleges in Chennai and Mumbai, while one or two were even going to Oxford and Cambridge.

"Don't move so much Ahalya," Kannappachettan said so loudly that everyone in the room even stopped their thoughts, and she, her internal dialogues. He had just begun to apply the first coat of *manayola*, that special pigment, and the *chayilyam* that gave a yellowish-orange sheen to the faces of female performers like herself. She was not 18 as yet, and she was bound to be restless, he told himself. But the older Chakiyar would have none of it, and had walked out in a huff once when he discovered that the young Ahalya was not reciting the Sanskrit verses with their *ragas*, with the correct intonation.

"Ah, Appa has now banned me from speaking in Hindi because he says it will affect my Sanskrit diction," she cried, hugging her mother one evening. She had been fond of Hindi films, and when they could, on the one free Sunday in a month in Kodaikanal, would go to watch these films. This they did even if by the time they were released in that small hill station, the hero in Mumbai had moved on to another hit film, and the heroine, had probably got married and retired from the industry itself.

She couldn't find that many CDs of Hindi films in this little village where she now lived, but what was to prevent her from watching *Roman Holiday*, her favourite film, a CD of which was in her collection?

"Ahalyakutti, if you twitch and move your mouth so, I certainly won't be able to finish your make-up even by tomorrow evening. You know how important this play is for Guruji, considering it is a play by Kalidasa that the Chakiyars don't perform often," Kannappa said, trying hard not to raise his voice. Guruji was hard on the girl as it was.

Ahalya was still young, and yet to get into the rigour of discipline this theatre tradition demanded. The Chakiyar had known no other way of life, and he expected these young children to be like him. For years on end, the Chakiyar had done nothing but read the *Ramayana* and *Mahabharata* in Sanskrit, and that too with two sticks placed under his arms to keep him awake. Or had spent whole mornings learning breath control. The Chakiyars were masters of breathing movements. It was said there was once a Chakiyar who held his breath for so long that the village thought he was dead, and summoned the *vaidya* in a panic.

Koodiyattam performances were sacred rituals held in the precincts of a *koothambalam*, the special theatre that many of the temples in these parts had. It was not a 'performance' in the sense the generation today understood it, Kannappa thought shaking his head with some desperation.

Who, for instance, would devote a whole life to learning this dance-drama form only to be allowed to go on stage after completing several years of study, by which time they would have reached the age of 30, if not more?

It was certainly not like the cinema of these days, where anyone with a beautiful face could become an actress without an hour's training in acting or dialogue delivery, he mused.

"This child is so good looking, and with such large eyes too. I just hope she has the patience," Kannappa was thinking aloud looking at the young Ahalya with affection.

He had been with the *gurukulam* for years and years now, and besides working at make-up which was as complicated in Koodiyattam as in Kathakali, he often played the part of the *vidushaka*. A journalist from London who was writing about their tradition, once commented that there was no one quite like Kannappa for the part of the archetypal jester, so mobile was his face. At other times, he was the administrator and the organizer, seeing that everything went well before and during a performance.

Ahalya was dreaming, after having watched *Roman Holiday* for the tenth or so time, that she would one day be able to go to Rome.

And that she would find a handsome man like Gregory Peck who she would fall in love with. She found some sort of companionship in Rama Varma, who performed with her these days. But, whom she had really liked was Amitabh from her high school days in Kodaikanal. He was such a handsome young boy, tall and athletic, like a Jane Austen character.

"Want to learn riding, Ahalya?" he had once asked, and she had been afraid wondering how she would ride in her ankle-length *pavadai*, the only clothing she was allowed to wear when she was out of school uniform. Amitabh, who was from a royal family, of Cooch Behar or somewhere else in Bengal, was planning on going to Oxford for his Bachelor's degree, and one day, becoming an international polo player.

She shook her head vigorously to shake off her dreams. How did it matter now to her what Amitabh was going to become? Considering she had not spoken more than a few words to him. And this only to say she could not learn horse riding for the moment, nor could she visit him in his royal estate, as she was expected to concentrate on theatre training once she was back home.

Who asked her anything about the life she wanted to lead or the things she wanted to pursue? She let out a sigh. The only thing she was repeatedly asked was: have you drunk your cup of Bournvita? Have you had your ritual massage?

"Chettan, you have known me since I was a child. Why didn't you at least ask me what I wanted, and who I wanted to become?" she wanted to open her eyes and ask Kannappa.

Kannappa was becoming angry as Ahalya was moving about too much. He was now drawing those elaborate and minutely detailed lines around her eyes with lamp soot (nothing was modern in these *kalaris*) and he didn't want her fluttering her eyelashes or opening her eyes this moment. This painting of the face was important in Koodiyattam for it allowed the actor to *become* the part they were playing.

This was the first time they were performing *Abhijnana Shakuntalam* with Ahalya. They would not be doing the whole of Kalidasa's play, which would, if done elaborately, take several nights to narrate. But then this 2000-year-old drama tradition had no beginning or end. And a Koodiyattam performance could begin at any point of the story, and go on for however long.

For that night's performance of two hours, they had chosen the episode when Shakuntala appears in the court of Dushyanta asking him to accept her as his queen. But since she was cursed by the sage Durvasa, the king would have no memory of her or the time they had spent together in the forest. How could he, she would plead with him, not recognize her, the woman brought up in sage's ashram; she, who was carrying his child? How was she to know that without the signet ring the king had given her, there was no means by which he would recognize her?

Ahalya shut her eyes tightly because tears were ready to well up in them, and she knew *chettan* was getting angry at her restlessness. She had wanted to go to a college, but her parents gave her no choice, when they told her she had to inherit the mantle of this theatre tradition.

Her father was no more, so this *gurukulam*, Kannappachettan, Chakiyarappa, her Amma, and now Rama Varma were all the family she had. She had wanted at least go to Thiruvananthapuram to do her Bachelor's in English. But with the weight of such a hoary tradition on her shoulders, how could she even say aloud that there were other things she wanted to do with her life than devote her life to a drama-form that her parents considered sacred? To make things difficult for her, UNESCO had recently declared this dance drama form as a world heritage. How could she be so irresponsible then, to say all that she wanted to do was to go to a college like other normal girls of her age? And one day marry someone like Amitabh?

Ahalya did not even have a moment to herself now that she had decided not to go college but live in the *gurukulam* with the other performers. Their schedules were packed from the minute they woke up at 4 am, and had a bath (at least they were not expected to go to the river to have their daily bath the way Chakiyar did at the age of 87). They then went for yoga and Sanskrit classes, and before lunch, had to sit with Chakiyar to learn *abhinaya* and storytelling. Or together they would read a Sanskrit text that laid out the rules of this tradition that Appa would ask her to write down in long hand, word for word, in one notebook after another! Appa never smiled in approval nor ever gave them an encouraging nod. But she had decided, if he didn't say anything, at least it meant they had got it right!

She wondered where Amitabh was now. Whether he had managed to go to Oxford, and whether he had become a polo player. If only the Internet connection was a little more reliable in these parts, she would have tried to get in touch with him by email.

She was sure she would find him and, unlike Dushyanta, Amitabh would still remember her.

For certain he would remember her as the girl who wore traditional skirts and blouses, but who nonetheless had the great classics of English literature. And had just begun to read James Joyce. *Ulysses* was impossible to complete even if she didn't have Sanskrit classes. But she was determined to finish it, for what were the difficulties of stream of consciousness novels, compared to her training as a Koodiyattam artiste where she had to learn everyone's parts in *Abhijnana Shakuntalam* by rote, not just hers alone? And not just for this one play, but for every play that was in the art form's repertoire!

If she found Amitabh's email ID, she would tell him all about the life she was leading now. It was a difficult life, yes, and even if it was a life thrust upon her. But she had become the torch-bearer of a vanishing tradition that would make her father proud of her, and shower flowers on her, as if she were a character in a mythological film.

Ahalya's make-up was now complete. Kannappachettan was handing over the dried pistil of the *chundapuvu*, which she would now drop into her eyes to make them red. She put the mustard-seed sized flower into her eyes, and closed her eyes in prayer: "Krishna, make me the Shakuntala that Appa will be proud of."

Shortly afterwards she walked up to the stage where the *mizhavu* drummers were sounding the plaintive note, which Guruji said was a way of summoning the gods to witness the performance.

Ahalya walked up to the centre of the stage where the lamp was lit. And began the parley with the fire that represented king Dushyanta: "Dear king, you who have fathered my child, how can you not remember your Shakuntala or the delightful times we spent together in the sage's forest?"

At the moment when the drama was all on her face and in her slight frame, it seemed there was no Ahalya. Only the sorrow of a bewildered Shakuntala.

There was not even the presence of a forgetful king. There was only the energy of the fire, and a woman who had found her space beyond the proscenium where she was performing.

ROAD NO. 3, BANJARA HILLS

IT HAD BEEN raining the whole night drenching not only the streets but also the mango and guava trees in the garden. The Flame of the Forest in the park a little beyond the compound wall had swayed uneasily in the stiff gale of the previous night. Rahul wanted to burrow into the warmth of his comforting *razai* and not wake up for another hour at least.

He remembered this was the day the family was moving out of the house, the only home he had known since he was a child. The transport truck was waiting at the gate, with the workers honking and hollering to be let inside. Rahul heard the commotion and, for a minute, speculated whether he should get up and go open the gate, but decided against it.

His mother would anyhow ask Allaudin, the driver or the maid Lakshmi, to do it. He buried his face in the pillow with the cool Superman cover on it that had been his since childhood. He felt a little silly holding on to it, but he needed, even felt comforted today, by the familiar things from his childhood.

"Rahul, *Ra-huu-l*, where are you?" his mother cried. She was in a frenzy as she wanted to reach the new house at the auspicious time given by the priest.

"Where are you Rahul? We have to move today and the least you could have done was not to go out with your friends last night, so that you could have gotten up early to help us with the moving," she said. She had begun winding up the house almost a month ago, and Rahul's was the only room she had left until the last hour.

When his mother had said she would clear the room, Rahul had protested, afraid that she would throw away something he might want to keep.

"I'll do it Ma, you don't worry, *na*," he had said almost every evening when he came back from school, before getting into his shorts to go out to play football at The Banjara Football Club that he believed was the best in all of Hyderabad.

"And the number of shoes you have, Rahul. That itself will occupy a whole truck," his mother yelled as a parting shot.

He had grown tall now, quite the handsome young man. But he had been just nine when his father, who everyone said he increasingly resembled, had passed away. He remembered the day they had brought his father home.

The 15th of April. It had been a cruel month for the family. He heard someone argue that the body should be kept in the garage of the house until the cremation so that the young children did not have to see a dead father.

Young as he had been he had wanted to say, hey, he is not the family car to be put away in the garage, he's my Pa. And what is dead, he had asked his older cousin Manu. More important, "Manuanna, will we still be related even if my Pa is not there?" he asked. After all, Manuanna was from his father's side of the family, and he really liked him because he could spin a top like no one else.

Manu had hugged him then and said things would be alright.

His little head was full of worries though. Who, for instance, would pay the rent for the house they loved so much? And what about the fees for the school, much as he hated it. Would they be able to afford his education?

He went to his sister and asked her, "Do you think we should run a phone booth to make money, or maybe run an *auto*?"

His sister, Rishika, a little older than him, was 12, and even more practical. "Sure, with the all the problems we have of drivers quitting constantly, who is going to run the autorickshaw? You?" she had smirked.

She was feeling especially important that day as everyone was wanting her to do some chore, and there was even talk of uncles and aunts taking them out to buy them clothes and other gifts.

Guests and visitors were being nice to the children. Rahul had never got as much attention as he did that day. That evening, everyone he knew, and didn't know, had either given him a hug or patted him on the head affectionately.

People had constantly asked him if he had eaten. How many times would he eat in a day? Besides, in the past, all that they had asked him was if he was doing well in school, and if he stood first in class like his sister.

Everyone assured the family that things would be alright. Except his best friend, Raj, who told him if they couldn't afford the big house anymore and had to move out, Rahul could stay with them in their house.

"We even have a tree house and we can sit there watching birds and snakes in the garden," Raj had whispered to Rahul.

Raj felt bad for his best friend. Worse, he thought if Rahul took up a part-time job in the evenings, he wouldn't be able to see him that often. And with whom would poor Rahul go for the football matches that he loved so much? Maybe his dad could take both of them.

There had been a stream of visitors that day, more than Rahul could ever remember in the house. More than even for the best ever birthday he had had last year when his mother had organized a clown, and a camel ride for everyone.

He had been playing with his dinosaurs underneath the staircase where he had built a huge Jurassic kind of park with sand, rocks, waterways, and trees, when he heard his name being called out. "Rahul, Rahul, we need you here."

Everyone was circling his father's body. They asked him and his sister to go around their father and touch his feet. "Akka, I don't want to go around Pa like this. I am feeling nauseous, Akka, please," he whispered to his older sister who was being led by their aunt.

He really wanted to go back to his dinosaurs. He had to feed them. His father was dead, he still didn't know what it meant, but his Pa looked as if he would get up, shave and go to office soon.

If he did get up, Rahul imagined, maybe he would take both of them to the new Superman movie as he had promised. The movie they never did go to, as on that very day his office had called him for a meeting.

Pa was the best in the office and was a senior president of the finance department. He liked the office where he would go on Sundays with his father and reorganize his papers and pens on the desk. He liked it more when Rishika didn't tag along.

He just wished his father had not spent so much time in the office. On Sundays he would promise to take them to the zoo or to the movies along with Raj and any of his other friends he might want to bring, but by breakfast time would announce that he needed to go for a meeting.

He didn't even make it to Rahul's sports day last year to see his son welcome everyone in the parade he was leading. He had called Rahul's mother in the afternoon to say he had to go out of town.

But Rahul liked it on the days when his father came home early. They both watched Michael Jordan shoot a basket, or a tennis match that he was not so interested in, but which he watched anyway because he could sit by his father and watch him smoke his pipe.

His mother would sometimes pretend to be mad with his father that he was ruining not only his health but also that of the young boy. Setting such a horrid example, she would say, hurrying both of them for the dinner that was set on the table.

But he wouldn't want to eat. Rahul would want to continue to sit in the crook of his father's shoulder, watching the smoke rise from the pipe.

They would be sitting in the living room of the house that contained a lot of his mother's artefacts, which she liked to bring from wherever she travelled. She didn't like it that they sat on her newly upholstered sofa and ate chips and drank juice. She disapproved of aerated drinks. She had even told Rahul there was no way she was going to keep them in the fridge.

But since Rahul and his father had so little time together, she let them be, even if she did get upset with the crumbs fallen all over the place when they were done with the television.

Now their beloved Pa was lying on the floor of this room; the chairs and tables had been put away to a corner, and the carpet rolled up. Rahul wanted to leave the room that had become claustrophobic with that many people and the priests chanting *mantras* he didn't understand.

Where was Raj? Where was his mother? He wanted to go to his secret hiding place in the back of the yard where he had built pathways of water, in which leaves and ants would float. He had even seen a snake here, in the chaos of overgrown trees and untrimmed bushes. But he had not told anyone. When he tried telling his sister, she had brushed him away, more interested in talking to her best friend, Nina, on the phone.

Rahul managed to escape into the garden. There he sat, for a while under the guava tree before he began to dig a pit in the ground. He buried one of his favourite dinosaurs here. He put a small branch to indicate that a dinosaur had been buried here, or else the silly gardener would stomp all over the place while sweeping the yard, walking over everything that he had built.

"Rahul," his mother was calling him again. "We are going to leave you in the house if you are not packed in five minutes," she said, asking Rishika to help Rahul with the packing of his cartons.

But Rahul didn't want Rishika or anyone else to come to his room that morning. He wanted to sort out things by himself.

Alone.

He began to pack all his childhood toys, video games and books in one carton, in another his clothes. Of what was remaining – all the postcards his father had sent him when he travelled to Europe, a red sweater of his father's that he had taken from the bundle his mother was giving to the Sisters of Charity – he put in another box that he told his mother he would carry in the car with him.

Then he put his ear to the walls of his room, listening to the sound of his father's voice and the stories of his life. The house echoed his little secrets. The missing feeling he had of Pa. That aching void and loneliness he felt every time he saw other boys go out to a restaurant with their fathers *and* mothers, not just with a mother, as he and his sister had been doing for so many years now.

When he got into the car with the two huge cartons, he didn't turn back to look at the house even once. He finally realized that life would never be the same again.

AMETHYST

HE LIT HIS cigarette, took a deep puff, snuffing the match into the ashtray. He was on Park Street, in one of the tea rooms that were all the rage with young people.

He had, in fact, come to the bookstore as he often did, especially when he had a free evening, but since it had begun to rain heavily all of a sudden, he had decided to stay back in the store and order a Darjeeling. His signature. Just like some men liked single malts.

He flipped open the large menu card, quickly glancing through it, finding everything from iced tea to latte, but not the Darjeeling. He looked up to ask one of the girls flitting about the restaurant in a short skirt, what else could he get at this hour.

But he was momentarily distracted because with the rain there was now thunder; the nor'westers that he had been so afraid of as a boy, along with other things. Of being by himself on a dull overcast evening such as this one. Or the frustration of having to locate someone who would get him his Darjeeling the way he liked to drink it – leaves in a strainer, floating in a cup of hot water. The water neither too lukewarm nor too hot, so that the tea retained the special aroma of the leaf.

He was a fastidious man.

That's what his daughter had told him a few days ago. A waif-like girl, who had taken up fashion designing instead of a proper career like everyone else. She had her children and their homework. The three meals a day she had to cook.

He wished her well. But found that he was becoming detached from the responsibilities of someone else's family. Even his daughter's. He did not even fully listen when his friends at the Bengal Club spoke about a son migrating to America or a daughter having to get married soon and the need to find a groom. He was over and done with that stage of his life.

Once was enough. He had been a sales manager in a biscuit company, driving to work in a Fiat, returning home to Alipore every single day of his working life for so many years that he even stopped counting.

Sometimes when he had had the time, he would stop at Flury's to pick up chocolates for his daughter. He had been a man trapped in his destiny. And there came a point when he wanted nothing more than to be the responsible man, who was at least good to his family. That ideal husband that people spoke of approvingly.

He looked at the button that was coming off his blue-checked shirt. Was this what he had chosen to wear this morning, he asked himself, surprised. At one time, he had been particular about his shirts too – the brands that he wore and the cufflinks that went with them. And the Montblanc that always sat snuggled in every one of his shirt pockets.

He looked around, disinterested, when he caught sight of an elegant woman in a green Dhakai sari talking animatedly to her companion. From the distance of his table he could not fully hear what she was saying. But there was softness in that voice. It was kind. Like this rain on a hot summer afternoon.

He noticed her neck, long like a heron's. Her hair in a tight chignon pulled up as if she had removed herself from the world. She did not wear any jewellery, neither earrings nor bangles.

As one of the girls in a short skirt finally came to take his order, his eyes fell on the woman's neck, the hollow at the base of her throat, as she looked towards him and their eyes met briefly before she turned away.

And he saw the amethyst pendant dangling from a thin silver chain. After so many years.

The rain didn't let up but he got up to leave the tea room. For now, at least, he did not want to know if he had known her in another lifetime. Nor did he attempt to jog his memory. Even love was a thing of past.

TALK TO ME

SWEETHEART, CAN WE sit on that bench, under the trees? I am tired from walking around.

Walking around? Where did you walk? It's just 20 minutes to Raffles. Do you want to eat now?

But we just had breakfast. When did I say hungry? I said tired. How come you don't know the difference? You never listen to me. And this heat is getting to me.

But this is Singapore, dear. It's going to be warm, though it's not as warm as I expected it to be. And a little sun is good for you. Vitamin D.

It was raining last night. Did you hear the rain, doc?

It did?

Well if you didn't sleep so much, you would have noticed.

Yes *memsahib*, I slept. Guess it's the jetlag. Did you not sleep?

What are you mumbling in those undertones? I can tell you,

your eyes closed from day, or shall we say night one. Never known anyone so tired. Guess it's because of all the weekends you work. And the calls you are on, whenever I am trying to reach you!

Whatever you say, *memsahib*.

Don't 'memsahib' me now. Can we just sit under those tall maple or whatever trees they are and admire the lovely hotel? So historical. Why do we need to rush around?

Yes, let's. We can sit on the bench and admire the world. That's what old people do.

Old?

You are not old. I am.

Look, that elderly couple is getting up and leaving, seeing that we are sitting here. Guess they are from America – that twang is from Midwest isn't it?

And look at this fellow, the gardener. He is so good. Going around trimming the trees with such grace. Like a dancer with his rhythmic movements.

But he's paid for that. That's his job.

Well, I pay my gardener too in Bangalore, and all he does is sleep under the shade of the mango tree.

Singapore is like that. They will water the trees at a particular hour of the day. Everything is done by the book here.

Yeah, I heard each tree is recorded and documented. Wish they did that in Bangalore. We used to have such old trees. Jacarandas and Raintrees. All gone now, or going... What are those shoes you are wearing? And yellow too. Are they walking shoes?

My dear, I have worn these for the last two days. How come you notice them now?

Hmm, I did notice them a long time ago. Meaning to ask you. Are they for walking around? Or lounging around?

Both actually. But you are always so well turned out. Like a Hindi filmstar.

Filmstar? A Bollywood one that too? Don't try to flatter me. It's not going to get you anywhere.

Anywhere? But it got you to Singapore! And to my bed.

Yes, that it did! Was I any good? I've lost practice you know!

It's not about practice. Anyway, you could teach Hugh Hefner's bunnies a thing or two.

Me? What are you saying? But I am still not sure how you convinced me to come to Singapore. What a crazy idea to fly here. Just like that.

It was not just like that. You had to go and book your ticket. Besides, I wanted to see you.

So did I. But to think I would fly that many hours to come to see someone I had lost touch with for 10 years. I must be mad. Is it 10?

I don't know. I can't remember anything now. Not drinking enough ginseng tea these days.

What does ginseng have to do with the number of years we didn't meet? Anyway, when was it? I know it was during Christmas. And did you see the streets last night? On Orchard Road, so pretty with Christmas lights.

The streets were pretty with all blue and pink lights. I know you liked them. The way you stood and stared.

That's okay. I was asking you when did we meet last? Remember?

Dear, I can't remember.

And if you say you don't even remember meeting me, I am going to go home right now.

Home to Bangalore or to the hotel?

No point asking you anything. Impossible to have a conversation with you. I am going to stay quiet.

Do you want to eat anything at Raffles? We can eat at the Tiffin.

I said I am not going to say anything. Besides we just ate an hour ago.

Eat again. The food here is nice. I might just be able to order the *dosa* for you.

Sweetheart, I don't want to eat a *dosa*. Not in Singapore anyway. I eat that every other day in Bangalore.

But it could be part of the many things you did here with me.

Wow, eating *dosa* with the world famous doctor! Why do you zip around the world like that?

Work, dear. I am not creative like you. So, I have to be the coolie.

All that cheesecake and mousse you are making me eat... Surely, I must have put on five kilos in the last few days. What do you think? Have I put on weight? Do I look the same after all these years? You've gone down, you know. Working too much. You need someone to take care of you.

You still look as lovely as the first day I met you. No, you haven't put on any weight. Not in the places I held you.

Why do you shuffle around the room like that in the mornings?

I was trying to find plug points for the chargers. For the phone.

And the Mac or whatever you use. Wish you had stayed in bed with me.

I did. What's wrong with wanting to charge the phone?

Nothing is right about it either. But you are a famous doctor, so I guess people must want your advice all the time.

Why didn't I see a message from you in my inbox?

Silly, I was with you. Why would I want to send a mail? And to think after all those mails you send you don't even talk to me.

But, I am talking to you. Do you want to go to the Tiffin?

Not unless you want to go.

What do you want to do?

Nothing. Just hold my hand. Is that a punishable offence in this country?

No, only spitting and chewing gum are. You are not chewing any, are you?

Noooooooooo!

There's no need to get hysterical. It's bad for your heart. Let's go check out the museum at the hotel.

But you told me once you hated museums!

If you want to go, I will too.

You are so sweet. Such a darling.

The museum was something, dear. So interesting. Did you see that poster about how they make the Singapore Sling? Swish, swish and some cherry brandy. Nice.

It was at Raffles that the Singapore Sling originated. Did you know? If you liked the museum so much why did you walk out so fast? Why the big hurry?

I can't walk like you. And Somerset Maugham sat at this bar writing books like *Of Human Bondage*. You should know better. I don't know anything about books and writers.

Doctor knows who Somerset Maugham was, ha? You just act dumb. You know everything.

Come, let's look for the bar. Let me show it you.

You've been here before, it looks like.

No, just had a drink some time ago. I want to stay here some-time. Everything is so Raj here.

You are not going to ask me to come again to Singapore? That's alright!

What did you say? You want to come here again? To Raffles. Alright.

Well, the sun has set on the Empire. But here it's all so British. I bet all these American tourists love it. The notion of the Raj. I bet you love it too.

I am not American.

But you live there.

Yes, I do. Let me look for the bar.

We've been around the hotel three times already. But no sign of the bar. Let's give it a miss.

Shall we go to the Tiffin?

No, let's go to the mall.

Whatever you say.

You don't want to go? Don't sound so resigned and bored. Do you have things to do? Phone calls?

I always have work. Looks like one of my patients is going to have a heart attack. But for now, I will do whatever you want me to do.

The inability of the doctor to distance himself from his patients. Am I making sense?

Eh, what?! I am wondering which way to go to Orchard Road.

We are walking?

You want to take a taxi?

I don't know. We have to figure how far it is.

Let's take the train. Which shop did you want to go to? What do you want to buy?

I don't want to buy anything.

You don't want to go then?

Did I say I don't want to go? I want to. But I don't have anything particular in mind. For this trip, I am happy that we reconnected. That's about it.

You should go the National Museum.

Only if you will go with me.

Go when I am sleeping. I wouldn't know you were not there. Did I say anything wrong? I never know what upsets you.

National Museum can go to hell. And don't ask me what I want to buy. Women go shopping not because they want to buy something, but because they like to see what's new in the stores. It's in their DNA.

Now, watch the street when you are crossing, darling.

You are like a typhoon. Wish you wouldn't walk so fast. I literally have to run behind you. And in bed too. I have to chase you all over the bed to be able to hold you.

Chase me? My beauty, you occupied three-quarters of the bed. Next time, I will ask for a larger bed.

If there is a next time.

Did you say something, dear?

Nothing. Can we stop by at the café in the mall?

Ah, at last you want to eat something?

I need to recharge myself with a drink.

Have iced tea?

What will you have? I will have the soda.

I will just have a glass of water.

That's it? You are so strange.

Why are you so tired?

You will never understand. You don't know anything about the heart, you world famous doc of the heart.

Tell me.

No. It doesn't matter.

C'mon. I want you to talk. You will feel better.

I should talk? What else have I been doing?

And I am listening… young lady, I am all ears.

Don't mock me!

Would I dare to? What is troubling you now? You know, I do want you to have a good time.

Ah, I just feel sad about the distance that separates us. Who knows when I will see you again?

I have a busy schedule back at the hospital. How do I make you understand?

Did I ask you to abandon all that? When did I say that? But tonight, you will go back to your life and I to mine. Wish I could run away.

You already have, dear.

Have I?

You are silly. We will meet.

Where? In my dreams?

Don't get so petulant.

Petulant? Who? Me? I am supposed to feel happy about this?

Why do you have to be so emotional?

How will you know what I feel?

Let's go back to the hotel. I am expecting some calls.

Alright. Let's go. Let's walk.

Don't be so ill-tempered. I'll call for a taxi.

Don't walk so fast. I am not an athlete like you. And I am wearing heels, if you didn't notice. Not those comfy walking shoes that you are wearing.

After you, my dear.

At least it's cool in the room. What are you going to do now?

Need to check my mails. Then, will go for the sauna.

Sauna? What's this obsession with the sauna? You've been going on since morning. Since the day we arrived, in fact.

It opens up the pores. It's good for the skin. You should try it too.

Forget it. Go sit in the sauna as long as you want to.

Let me get the steam going then.

That's all you are interested in. Let me also go and pack then. I might as well.

I will be back in 20 minutes, darling.

Take your time.

Ha, there you are. Smelling like freshly-washed laundry too.

Laundry? Darling, did you give some of your clothes to housekeeping?

Never mind, I said you smell nice. Was the sauna good? Now, can you come and sit next to me. Just for a few minutes before we leave.

Dear, don't look so sad. What's there to be sad about?

I just wish we didn't have to leave. I don't want to go. I don't want to leave you. God in heaven help me. And save me from this doctor who doesn't understand anything I say!

Shall I get the sauna going for you? Or how about a soak in the tub? It will calm you.

I don't need the sauna or the tub bath. I would feel calm if you hugged me.

You should write. Did I inspire you to write?

You inspired me to have a baby. Shall we?

Eh, what? I thought you already have one of your own.

Do you have to take everything so literally, doc?

Do you want to eat before we check out of the hotel? We can eat in the business class lounge too.

Sweetheart, hold me for a minute. Talk to me. Say something!

A PIECE OF MY HEART

MALLIKA LOOKED OUT of the window of her apartment. She sighed wistfully for not having anyone else to share her sense of wonder. She had never felt so alone than at this moment, when darkness and night were descending on Manhattan. The city had unfurled itself to another evening of conversations. And would now light up simultaneously, a light here, another there, until literally the whole of Manhattan would be drowned in the fluorescent glow of a megalopolis.

Manhattan was a nocturnal city and everything seemed to happen in those imperceptible minutes, when the lights were turned on in individual apartments.

From an apartment nearby, she heard the faint sound of a Janis Joplin favourite, *A piece of my heart*. In this day of rap and hip hop who, she wondered, was listening to Janis. Joan Baez and Janis were of her generation. She remembered the time when she and her friends sat in Bangalore's Rex theatre watching the film on Woodstock festival. After that, they imagined they were in New York, or at least outside it, in Bethel where the festival had been held.

So keen was her identification with the festival that defined her youth that she had imagined her friends and she would live one day in communes, sleeping under the stars, listening to music. In those days. When getting a job was not of much concern to anyone.

In her imagination, she had even thought she would have a child outside of marriage, though she was not clear who the man would be, nor how she would pull this off with an orthodox, if caring, family hovering around her all the time.

Surely her mother would turn up for the delivery, even if she were hiding in Bethel, armed with homemade *lehyams* and *podis* for the combined health of the mother and child. She imagined her partner would be a poet or a singer, or someone who had at least burnt his draft card post-Vietnam.

But even in her wildest imagination, this south-Indian rebellion had its limitations. She would not use drugs that some of her friends were trying out.

What she did, as a mark of empathy with the flower children, was to get herself a pair of large round glasses (like Janis and Joan) and a metal peace-pendant which she wore around her neck on a black thread, disconcerting her family, especially her mother.

Her mother had wanted her to wear gold all the time. Not even silver. "*Daridram*, that you have to wear this cheap metal chain," she would scold urging her to wear the thin gold chain that she had bought recently. "And what are those filthy bellbottoms you insist on wearing every day of the week? I wish you would get them washed. Even Mangamma is asking if you will ever put them for a wash," she would say with contempt. Many times Mallika had to flee out of the backdoor in her favourite bellbottoms and dark glasses, looking like Zeenat Aman, post the *Dum maro dum* blues.

Mallika moved away from the window to stack the dishes into the washer in the kitchen. "Let's go to Bethel, Mallik. Please, sweetheart. I'll drive you up there. Don't be such a Jayanagar *maami*," Sand's words echoed in her ears. He was actually Sandip, but after migrating to America on an H1 visa he had changed his name to 'Sand'.

Well, she thought, he could go if he wanted to, but he couldn't expect her to be bohemian like him and not worry about dusting the furniture or making the *kootu* and deep freezing it for the week. At least, he could give her time till she vacuumed the house a little bit, and got some basics of cooking done.

Nothing like having chopped cabbage and *paruppu* in the fridge to make a nice *kootu* and *poriyal* for a weekday evening when they came back from work. These IT companies paid you good salaries, but you gave them your soul in the bargain, she thought.

There was so much work at both office and home that she sometimes forgot that she was in New York, which had been her favourite place in the whole world. It still was, she told herself firmly, despite everything.

"Mallik! OK, then, I will leave you to vacuum the apartment, or dust the books or put away the dishes," Sand would say and let himself out of the door, and go down the elevator into the crisscrossing streets that made up the city of New York.

After that, she would be so confused that she would not do the laundry, or vacuum or cook the *sambar* with the radishes that she had got from the grocers in Jackson Heights. Or if she did, she would cry into the laundry basket or, worse, the *sambar*. Until he called her from Greenwich or SoHo bar to say that he missed her.

But neither would he ask her to drop everything and come to the bar nor would he quit drinking and take the subway back home to be with her.

That was Sandipa, as she had liked to call him. After her disastrous marriage long ago, to someone her parents had arranged, she had sought refuge in an IT job, especially overjoyed that she was going to be sent to New York for two years.

When she found an apartment overlooking Manhattan across from the Hudson river, her happiness, it seemed, was complete.

Greenwich and Soho were just a subway journey away, the Metropolitan another breath away, and even the NYPL, yes, the great New York Public Library, was a reality now and not simply something to lust for when reading the *New York Times* online. She could now actually sit in its large hall and read a book, or better still, sit on its steps and feel like a New Yorker. Life, it seemed, couldn't get better.

But it did get better when Sandip walked into her life. He was a friend's brother, or more like 'cousin brother' as they say back home; except that this cousin brother had read all of Gabriel Marquez, Kafka and Lhosa, had sat in the Village many a time to drink the night away, and could interpret Brahms and Beethoven as if these great composers, and not Thyagaraja, were the legends on the street where he grew up, in Mandavali Gardens in Madras.

And he had done what she had always dreamt of – never got married, defied parents, quit a well-paying engineering job – to become a writer. She admired him for walking to the beat of his own drum.

When she met him, he had been between jobs, mainly smoking and dreaming. He said he had chucked his boring IT job to finish a novel on music, but he had never shown her any manuscript so far. She knew something about writing since her good friend, with whom she grew up in Bangalore, became a journalist. She had often told her how tough it was to be sitting in front of a computer and your mind going so blank that you were not able to write a single line.

It was a lot of hard work – her friend, who was moody most of the time, had told her. But with Sandip, she saw only a couple of aspects of a writer's life that she had heard about – cigarette smoke and the long spells of moody silence.

She was not sure whether she had invited him to share the apartment with her or whether he had just moved in with his books and clothes one night after they had made love.

When he walked in with his boxes that night, he had said the apartment made him feel comfortable. He loved to look at the moon over the Hudson from her window, he said, giving her a hug of familiarity. The kind you gave a long-standing girlfriend. From then on, it was *their* apartment.

Her happiness, as they say in third-rate romances, knew no bounds. She was so happy, in fact, that she invited family and relatives from India included, to visit her.

"I want to share this lovely apartment," she emailed to her friends and relatives from across the world.

Promptly, a distant aunt decided to take up the invitation, and arrived from San Jose with her daughter. This naturally sent Mallika into a tizzy, for she did not know how to explain to her conservative aunt that she and Sandip were partners.

After her divorce, her family had wanted her to remarry, no doubt, but a live-in relationship was not on the cards. Certainly not on the cards of a conservative, well brought-up, Tamil Iyer girl's life, anyway.

Her friend in India, whom she emailed and chatted regularly with, advised that she declare Sandip a colleague who was staying with her until his assignment in New York got over.

"Tell her you are trying to save money. Take it from me, nothing delights a Tam-Bram's heart more than money saved by cutting corners," she wrote back.

"Except," Mallika wrote back churlishly, "how the hell do you want me to explain his clothes in my cupboard, his shaving kit in the bathroom, and his shoes in the closet?" "I don't know," her friend wrote back. "It's your problem."

The visit went off better than she expected. Sandip played the perfect host, taking them shopping, to the Metropolitan, and for dinner at Tandoor, the Indian restaurant. She had to restrain him from buying tickets to Broadway, though. That would be taking generosity to the extreme. Besides, the aunt was too distant to impress so much.

But he was like that, the eternal charmer, and generous to the core. Everyone liked him. Even her aunt, who winked while departing to San Jose, and asked, "Is there something cooking between the two of you?"

Which was something Mallika herself could never figure out. Was there anything at all between them or was it only her imagination? When they made love, she felt she was dear to him. But when he withdrew like that after the love-making, to retreat from the room into the kitchenette or some other room, into himself even, she felt abandoned.

"I am working on the play Mallik. Why do you have to get uptight about everything?"

After that, in the morning, he would be standing before her with a tray of her favourite muffins and coffee. "Coffee, just the way my lady likes it, brewed the *Madrasi* style," he would say waking her up with a hug and letting his hands slide all over her again.

What was the love that she felt for him? Was it fascinating only because it seemed so fragile? She had not even valued her marriage at the height of its happiness as much as she did this relationship with a man who might walk in and out of her life as he pleased. She would not allow that, of course.

She should really stop working constantly on her laptop. Her clients in other time zones (the eternal bane of the software industry) really be damned. For once, she was not going to be on call.

Mallika got up, cleared the table of her papers, only to stumble on a photograph of Sandip and her taken at Ellis Island in a moment of childish happiness. He had his hand on her shoulder and she was giving her 1000-watt smile to the camera.

And looking at the photograph, she realised she could look quite radiant. Quite the New Yorker, really, in that lovely black skirt and silk blouse. Though her friend, on seeing the photograph as an attachment, had asked, "Mallika, what is that puff-sleeved blouse? Its *so* not New York!"

Ah yes, she had looked nice once. Not now, she thought, when she didn't want to look at herself in the mirror, and had once again picked up her college-time habit of smoking.

Smoking among women was on the rise in the world while men, for reasons of health, were all but giving it up, she had read somewhere. Just as she had read that there were more chances of live-in relations breaking up. These days, a mail forward had an answer to every issue that plagued mankind, she decided, getting up to look out of the window into Manhattan. Even at a depressing moment of her life, this island never ceased to fascinate her.

Mallika made up her mind to get out of her dowdy *salwar–kameez* that her mother would have approved of, but which Sandip hated. She would wear a nice skirt, dab some Chanel 5 perhaps, and bring out the red wine they liked to share. He was the one who trained her Iyer tongue into appreciating wine and telling the difference between a good, a mature and a young wine. He could even tell which vineyard the bottle came from.

At that time, all that she could tell was the difference between freshly ground coffee without chicory and one that came packaged as Nescafe 'fresh' coffee, whatever the word 'fresh' here meant, considering the coffee must be have been packed ages ago!

She would read his favourite poet; Neruda, who else? He would come back, she thought to herself as she hummed Janis. And when he did, she would go with him to Bethel and not make a fuss about vacuuming the house or cleaning and dusting the furniture.

Maybe they would even stay back at the farm, strum a few Crosby, Stills, Nash & Young songs, and sleep under the stars. She would, of course, take a sheet from home, and a nice picnic hamper of cucumber sandwiches and wine (certainly no *upma* or *idlis*, though she did debate if she should use some *pudina* chutney on the sandwiches).

New York had been her dream.

Everything she ever wanted in life was here. The books, the poetry, the music, NYPL, and who knows there was even a chance of bumping into Woody Allen who, it was rumoured, lived somewhere on Park Avenue.

Why had she morphed into a housewife when all she wanted to do was walk in New York's streets with Sandip, sit in the very centre of Times Square where, they say, if you sat long enough you would see all the people you ever knew?

Mallika felt a surge of energy at the thought of the bustling Times Square. But it was quite late. And she heard her mother's booming voice in the background, saying that well brought-up girls had to be home by dusk. The hour when the lamp was lit in the *puja* room of a traditional south Indian home.

For once, Mallika decided to set aside the anxieties that she carried from Bangalore, of girls like her not going out alone in the night.

This was New York pulsating with life even at this midnight hour. She would even dare to take the subway to Times Square. Surely, she would find a piece of her heart there.

THE MONA LISA SMILE

WHEN KIARA WOKE up, she realized she was alone at home, and remembered Malavika had said that she would leave early to catch the morning light for a photo shoot. She had asked her if she wanted to go with her, but as it was only two days since she had arrived in Paris, Kiara wanted to sleep in late. Especially after all those Margaritas Malavika and she had drunk the previous night.

Kiara decided to linger a while at home, make a cup of Brazilian coffee, have a quick shower and take the train to central Paris by late morning.

She walked around Malavika's less than 10x10 apartment, which was located in a really old building in Montmartre. The building was so ancient that there were no elevators, and when she arrived she had to walk up seven flights of wooden stairs with both her suitcases to the apartment perched on the penultimate floor. There was even an old water fountain on the ground floor, making her feel that this building could have been constructed during the time of Louis XIV or Marie Antoinette.

Even if the apartment was old and small, Malavika had said, it was an expensive place and she had taken it because she had wanted to stay in the heart of the art district of Paris, and did not mind paying the exorbitant rent.

"You must go up to the Basilica of Sacré-Cœur, the Catholic church up there," she advised Kiara. "It's a steep climb, but you will love walking on the cobbled stone streets, which you'll see when we go to the Moulin Rouge at night."

Sipping coffee from the mug that had the reproduction of a Picasso, of a man and a woman in Cubist distortions, Kiara began to browse through the apartment.

The morning was still young, and besides, there was no pressure of newspapers to be skimmed through, which had often held up the mornings in India, leaving little time for meditative thoughts or even foolish ruminations.

The apartment was just two rooms and a kitchen, but Malavika had brought her own sense of aesthetics to even this little space.

The kitchen was so clean, she wondered if Malavika ever cooked at home. There was a study-cum-dining area which also had stacks of music CDs, and a guitar standing in the corner. From here, she had a lovely view of the street below.

When Kiara opened the windows for fresh air (what was this obsession that newly-arrived Indians had for fresh air, she wondered) and looked through the potted geraniums on the sill (how did Malavika manage to water them?), she saw the streets being washed clean, by thick hose pipes from water tankers. She made a mental note to ask Malavika whether this was an everyday ritual in Paris.

She circled the apartment, looking at the black and white photographs on the walls. There were portraits of children and men. Of Parisian windows with flowerpots on their sills, and one of a cat curled up on a floor cushion with a beautiful abstract painting in the background.

There was one, of a man in the nude which Malavika kept in the bedroom, diagonally opposite from her small settee-like bed. Kiara was curious, but she realized that this was her friend's home and she had no business snooping.

However, she could not help leafing through Malavika's books, hoping to find a clue to the person Malavika might have become in the years they had been apart.

Besides books on photography and art, books on Paris, a coffee-table book on India, she found Marquis de Sade's writings, Henry Miller's novels, even an edition of the *Kamasutra*. In that instant, a strong sense of being an intruder overcame her. Like violating someone's private world by opening their letters.

Feeling guilty, she decided to quickly shower and leave the apartment. As punishment, she would not have the croissant Malavika had left for her in the kitchen, she told herself in some anger, even disgust.

She wore a floral dress with spaghetti straps and stepped out, pulling the heavy wooden door behind her. "Bang the door hard or it won't lock," Malavika had warned, and she closed the door harder, in her anger.

She felt all chic in her clothes, and with a name like Kiara she even felt French.

In reality she was Katyayani, a name that could not be more traditional, but which sometime during high school she shortened to Kiara; about the same time that she had started smoking cigarettes and acquired her first boyfriend (whose name at this point of time she could not recall). It was that far back that she had morphed into Kiara.

Her best friend was Malavika, to whom she had often suggested that she change her name to something more modern, like Lika or Mika at the very least.

"But, I'd rather not have a pet name," Malavika had protested. So Kiara and others had to address her by the name that Kalidasa had given one of his heroines. Even the stubborn Kiara was forced to concede defeat on this issue.

Back then when they were in their early years of college, they had hung out most of the time at Malavika's house, gossiping about one boy or another – who looked at them or who didn't. Or, who called them one day and didn't the next – making them stare at their telephones hungrily.

Once, they were in serious trouble with Malavika's mother, who found out from the maid that they had been smoking in the bedroom, and she warned Kiara to stay away from the house and not drag Malavika on to the devil's path.

Even then, Malavika had a large collection of eclectic books and music, which Kiara constantly borrowed and took home. Recently, she was surprised at the number of Malavika's books that were in her bookcases and cupboards. Books, with their bookmarks and the bits of papers with phone numbers, names and other scribbles that her friend had made.

In the shame she felt, she meant to bring some of them to return to Malavika. But either because she had not subconsciously wanted to, or because in the end, her bags were overflowing with sandals and dresses, she didn't carry the books.

She had even forgotten to tell Malavika that if she had been looking for her Simone de Beauvoirs and Anais Nins, they were with her.

Malavika had moved to Paris as an undergraduate student, and had stayed back to study theatre, supporting herself as a magazine photographer.

Forgetting that just a few hours ago she had felt a sense of guilt browsing through Malavika's books and photographs, she sat cross-legged in one of the street-side cafes in central Paris, reading Camus' *Outsider* while sipping a glass of red wine.

Kiara was not sure why she had picked up this book from the many in the apartment (was it because it was slim and would fit into her bag or was it that she wanted to see if she could find new meaning in it?). But there she was, in central Paris, reading the classic for the fourth or fifth time.

Her mind, however, would not let her forget the nude study she saw in the apartment. Was it Michael, Malavika's, boyfriend she mused, despite her resolution that she was not going to be curious about her friend.

Malavika had changed considerably. Kiara somehow did not feel she was in the presence of a friend with whom she had sat in dark cinema halls in Madras, cutting classes, to furtively watch *Becket* and *Cromwell*. And whispering how good-looking Peter O' Toole was.

Malavika had not written to her about Michael, so when both of them came to the airport to receive her, she thought that with his long ponytail and one earring he was another photographer with the magazine she worked with. But after dinner when he didn't leave, she realized that Michael and Malavika were partners.

She smiled kindly at the French waiter, a boy who seemed to be barely out of his teens. She wanted to tell him this was how

Sartre and Simone de Beauvoir, Gertrude Stein, Francoise Gilot and Pablo Picasso, Hemingway, Anais Nin, June and Henry Miller must have sat in the '20s and '30s in these very sidewalk cafes, drinking bottles of wine, arguing about art and politics, later going home to write or probably make love.

The young waiter, who must have been a high school student, probably did not even know who these people were, people that she and Malavika had grown up reading in college.

She had been fascinated by the nurturing relationship Sartre and Simone had shared, or the somewhat perverted relationship Miller and his wife June shared with Anais. Kiara imagined that one day she would meet a man who was a writer or a painter, and they too would sit in a Parisian café and sip wine.

For the moment, she was happy she had reached as far as Paris and had a name that a Frenchman or Italian could roll on his tongue, and say with love – Kiara.

Kiara felt satisfied at the thought, and in anticipation of all that was about to unfurl before her she ordered another glass of red wine and lit her cigarette, hoping it was not another non-smoking area that the world was infested with these days.

She had a moment of pessimism; but she decided she was not going to worry about things like creeping age or the ticking of the biological clock. or think about the likelihood of a woman above 45, ever meeting that one passionate lover.

Hadn't her yoga teacher told her not to be so pessimistic about life and to imagine only good things happening to her? 'Creative visualization' it was called in the books that the teacher, a frail lady with a high-pitched voice, had recommended between deep breathing and teaching her how to chant the *Yoga Sutras*.

This was what the yoga teacher had meant by creative visualization: not only did she have to think of Paris but feel the glow of having a French or Spanish boyfriend.

In honour of the pleasant Paris afternoon, she tried not to think of her job as a lecturer at the women's college in Madras.

Most times, seeing that none of the young girls could write one grammatically correct sentence in English, leave alone have any feeling for the poetry of Keats or Byron, she had fervently wished that all of them would listen to their mothers, find a suitable boy and get married. At least, they could make a man a good meal of rice and pepper *rasam*.

Rasam and rice didn't sound so cool here, given the Parisian ambience, so she kicked off her gladiator shoes and looked at the menu to see what she should order.

When you said legumes only, the waiters (the waitresses were worse) sized you up as if you were a creature from another planet that did not know what haute cuisine was, and turned their attention to other customers. Maybe she would order risotto and plead with them not to put oysters or scallops or whatever else that was not vegetarian on the menu. At least, in risotto she would have a whiff of the rice she was so used to eating.

And where was Malavika? She had told her she would meet her for lunch during the break if she got off her editorial meeting, but there was still no sign of her.

If she didn't come in the next few minutes, she would head for the Louvre. Too many things to be seen and ticked off her list of things to do in Paris, and so little time, even if it was a week she was going to spend here.

And one of the things she wanted to do (Mona Lisa certainly was not high on her list though she would quickly glance at the lady) was to spend time with Malavika and share all that had happened in their lives in all the years they had not been in touch.

How on earth did she meet Michael, for instance. He was good-looking and had such great manners that he could have been that one man, who tarot-card readers often promised would appear suddenly in your life and so extracted an extra tip from you.

Soon enough, between her second glass of wine and risotto, Malavika called to say that she would not be able to make it for lunch, but Michael was free and could he take her to the Louvre or the Musée d'Orsay or wherever she wanted?

Kiara thought to herself, she certainly would not mind Michael taking her out, though out of politeness she told Malavika that she was fine and she could manage the Louvre on her own.

"I mean, you guys must have seen it so many times, especially with every Madras visitor who must have passed through Charles de Gaulle airport," she told Malavika in Mylapore Tamil which they lapsed into frequently when they felt the bonding of girls who had grown up together.

Malavika was like that – substituting herself with someone close to her. When she could not make it to an event where her presence was required, she would send her mother or brother to be with them.

On Kiara's graduation day, she had sent her brother Sanjay. What Sanjay was to do with her after the graduation ceremony in a women's college neither Kiara nor her friend had completely thought through.

Everyone who had come to meet Kiara to congratulate her, as she had topped in a few subjects, looked at Sanjay as if he were a prospective groom, either for Kiara or for themselves. Young girls sometimes didn't get into the finer details when they saw single men like him.

To this day she couldn't forget Sanjay, with whom she couldn't even imagine a romance, and his discomfiture because everyone assumed he was her boyfriend. That he had married one of Malavika's friends from the advertising course was another matter.

"Not all friends of your sister's are as bad as me," she had said to him at the wedding, giving him a hug.

Michael called to ask where she was and told her to hang in there until he appeared. He would take no longer than half-an-hour to get to where she was. He was with his friends, putting together a gig.

Gig? When had Malavika become so bohemian, Kiara wondered. What would Sanjay and Vasanta aunty say about Michael?

Even if he is white (they would have preferred an Oxford-educated Britisher or even an American from Yale or Harvard; she was not sure how they would react to his Italian connections), they would have liked him to be a doctor or even a banker. Not certainly someone who was in the entertainment industry.

South Indian parents liked bankers and doctors as sons-in-law; maybe they felt that such men could provide their daughters a sense of security, Kiara concluded.

Yes, that's why she had married Shiv, a banker who was as nice as nice could be, and had given her the comforts and security of a good home. The car, the drivers and the maids. But there was a limit to his wanting to duplicate that life even during a holiday; they had to have the same brand of tea that they had at home even in Bali. Or his craving to read the online version of *The Hindu*, even in Miami. Or insisting they find a temple, even if a Buddhist one, on his birthday when they were in Japan.

Shiv was a well-off banker and good-looking in a nice, middle class Indian sort of way, the kind who wore detergent-washed sparkling white shirts and who was clean shaven most mornings.

But after some time, she could not take his monomaniacal interest in his work, or his other diversion – the stock markets. And he couldn't stand her unconventional ways.

She still remembered the afternoon when he found her pack of cigarettes in the bathroom or the time he found she liked having Martinis in the evening all by herself. Or his wrath when she refused to wear the Kanjeevaram silk his mother had given her for her birthday.

"She is your mother, you love her, and you should love her as the only son. I really don't have to wear the awful blue silk sari she gave, and that too on my birthday!" she had said and stormed out of the house, even though it was her birthday and there was a dinner party to follow.

When Kiara wanted to separate from Shiv, his mother began to weep as she had hoped for a grandson, and her father was upset too.

She could not even talk all of it out with Malavika, who had stopped writing to her for no particular reason, except that life sometimes separates good friends who get so caught up in the dilemmas of their individual lives that they no longer feel the need to call or write. It happens, and so, good friends grow distant though they remain in the heart.

But she was a free woman now, though with no inheritance or alimony (that she was too proud to ask for) it was a difficult life she led, working and taking care of her father, who now lived with her and was not always in good health.

Paris was a holiday she had given herself during the college break, determined to live it up for once in her life.

She bent forward to buckle the shoes she had taken off, when she saw Michael coming towards her.

Those around, including the waiter, thought that he was her boyfriend, especially as he moved quickly towards her and kissed her cheeks once this way and then that way, with more than ordinary affection.

He held her hand and said, "C'mon Kiara, where do you want to go? What can I show you of this great city of love so that you will remember Paris forever?"

Were all Italian men so exuberant or was it just Michael? In Madras, if someone were your friend's boyfriend or husband, they would not hold your hands the way he held hers.

Coming to think of it, even your own husband did not hold your hand, not hers certainly. If she asked Shiv to hold her after they had made love, he would ask, already half asleep, whether she did not know he had an important meeting with his board members the following day, and he couldn't function without his eight hours of sleep? It doesn't take eight hours to hold your wife she would tell him, but in the ten years of their marriage she gradually stopped arguing with him over this and anything else.

They had both turned away and slept. That was when she decided, if she were to sleep curled into herself she might as well sleep on her own, in her own bed without a husband who now felt like a stranger working his way all over her body.

Michael said, "Lady, let's head towards Louvre station," which itself she found enchanting, for the art on its walls. When they emerged out of the station, almost near the long lines at the glass pyramid at the Louvre, he confessed the pyramid-like dome had changed the character of the museum that he had been seeing since he was a boy.

But even before she could go to buy the tickets, he spotted someone making crepes and dragged her towards the kiosk.

"Would you like a chocolate or a strawberry crepe, Kiara? And, with or without ice-cream?" he asked.

When he saw that she was so undecided, he asked her, gently, "Kiara, shall I order for you? Why don't you go with the strawberry crepe with some ice-cream on it?"

"It would take days to go through the Louvre. Can I just show you its highlights?" he said buying their tickets and guiding her through various sections of the museum. They lingered at the work of Whistler, and Michael said facetiously, "See, how much he loved his mom. This could be the universal card for Mother's Day!"

Though the Mona Lisa was not high on her list of things to do in Paris, and in the time it took for them to reach the museum, she had felt a gnawing anxiety about the great work of art, for which people actually made the pilgrimage to Europe.

Just as she was getting tired of walking around the museum which seemed forever and more, she realized she had worn the wrong footwear for such a day of walking around, when they stopped dead in front of the Mona Lisa.

Some Japanese and other tourists were furiously taking photographs. She spied an IT techie from Andhra or Karnataka with his earnestness, and IBM bag, heavens, the kind she would avoid in Madras, who was showing his new bride (or so Kiara assumed was one) the Mona Lisa.

She noticed, the techie's wife was not only wearing a brightly coloured green *salwar-kurta* with gold sequins on the *dupatta*, but also Bata *chappals*. She sighed, thinking how smart the young girl was to wear sensible footwear to walk around the museum.

Moving a little away, she craned her neck to see the Mona Lisa, which was ensconced in a bulletproof frame. While stepping back to get to a vantage point from where she could see the painting, she stumbled and almost fell, except that Michael who was behind her, or beside her, she was not sure which, swooped to catch her and broke her fall.

"Do you know that Mona Lisa's smile is so enigmatic that one artist, trying to figure out who she was and why she was smiling like that, even committed suicide? My own theory is that Leonardo, whose father never really acknowledged his mother, may have modelled the Lisa lady on his mother's likeness," he explained.

"You think so, Michael?" she asked.

He smiled at her but only said, "I think it's time we left the museum. Let's go for a stroll on the Champs-Elysées, and I will buy something for my mademoiselle."

Buy her something? But what about Malavika?

He was certainly flirting with her, and a little flirting was alright but should she be encouraging him to flirt with her at all?

He now decided they should take the bus so that she could look at the streets of Paris.

"We must cycle once through the city," he said as he peered out of the window of the bus and saw groups of cyclists stop by the traffic light.

"Do you know we are getting environment-friendly now and you can hire and drop off a bicycle in whichever corner of the city you want to?" he remarked, continuing to look out of the window.

Cycle? She became worried about who he thought she was, for she had not cycled since high school when she had ridden the bike so fast that she had hit a lamppost and sprained her leg. She had been bedridden with a cast for a fortnight and that had concluded her cycling saga.

"Certainly, Michael, we must cycle around the city tomorrow," she said nonetheless.

What she didn't say was we should ask Malavika to take the day off and go with us.

He didn't mention Malavika either. In fact, throughout the afternoon he had not mentioned his partner even once.

They stopped by all the windows of designer stores whose names like Prada, Gucci and Vertu if she let drop, her colleagues in college – Mrs Sundaram and Ms Ramya Krishna – would die of envy so pure, just like the ghee they were eternally searching for.

Kiara was hesitant to go into the designer stores, but Michael was full of confidence and took her to all the watch and jewellery stores, even asking her to try some watches while pretending to buy her a Cartier.

He told the sales girl (who looked so fashionable that Kiara hid the Titan watch on her wrist) to keep the watch aside as they would come back later to buy it.

He behaved as though she were his girlfriend. Even if this was only a charade, she went along.

"I want to take you to one more place before we head back to the apartment. It's a surprise, but I will take you if you will walk a little distance with me. The walk is pretty because we will be walking by the Seine," he said looking at her, hoping that she would walk with him.

When they walked for what seemed to her a half-hour, he brought her before Shakespeare & Co, that famous secondhand bookstore, which had been home to many an impoverished student and writer.

"Oh no, Michael, how did you know this is what I wanted to see, even more than the Mona Lisa!" she said. Now it was her turn to give him a delighted hug.

They wandered around the small store looking at the old and

new books and she could actually feel the presence of all those students and writers who must have slept here for a night, thanking George the owner who, Michael said, had now become old and was not to be seen around.

She picked up Richard Ford's *Multitude of Sins*.

He wanted to pay for it but she wouldn't let him do that. But she let him buy the bookmark that said 'Shakespeare & Co', for a euro. She would treasure not just the book, but also the time they had spent here. Thinking of that, she smiled at him and squeezed his hand with affection.

They reached home quite late in the night. Malavika was not back as yet. Michael opened a bottle of wine, and poured some into their glasses. While he cooked pasta for them, she made the garlic bread with a lot of cheese.

When she stood close to him drinking wine, he told her she had a lovely smile. Not enigmatic, with pursed lips like the Mona Lisa's. But inviting, he said tenderly, lifting her face towards him.

It was a make-believe world, she concluded. And she was going to live all of it, even if she knew she was entering another woman's world.

A CHARACTER IN SEARCH OF A WRITER

TAMAARA IS IN love with an idea. The idea of a writer called Arawinda Sena.

When one afternoon, browsing in the bookshop that had newly come up near her office, she picked up a novel called *Faith*. She wondered how she had not read even one review of the book in the newspapers.

She usually scanned the papers on Sundays to look up the new and worthwhile books in the market that she ought to be reading. She still liked to read fiction, though many of her colleagues didn't read anything other than self-help books like the ones about how to lose weight in one month, or how to give up your Ferrari and live like a monk.

When she came across a book that she thought she should read, she would write down its title and the name of the author in the little book in which she wrote notes to herself.

Many times, she forgot the beautiful handbook, which was bound in embossed camel leather (picked up in the by lanes of Udaipur), at home and never had it handy when she went to a bookstore, but that was another matter. Some people, she realized, wrote notes to themselves on their cell phones, but these were among the things she had not figured out in life.

Though she had not read anything about the book (maybe it was reviewed, and she had missed reading the Sunday paper those weeks she was away on a holiday), she liked the cover.

It was matte-finished, white on the outside with just the silhouette of a woman in black. A voluptuous Marilyn Monroe in a moment of abandon as it were. She saw the author's name. Arawinda Sena. He was a Sri Lankan writer who lived in California now, teaching at Stanford, the book jacket said. And then she saw the black and white photograph – piercing eyes, a graying exuberance of hair, and beard.

She stared back at those eyes and asked herself who he was, who so stunned her that she decided to buy the book impulsively, though the hardbound edition was way above her budget.

It was Rs 800 – a lot to pay for a book, when she still had to pay the house rent and was saving to upgrade her laptop. Ideally, she should have waited for its paperback version or asked her friends to pool in and buy it as a gift for her birthday.

But an inner voice urged her to get the book, saying, "Tamaara, why do you have to think so many times before buying a book? It's your money. Remember when you were young? All that you wanted was to earn enough so you could buy books, and not have to wait for a birthday?"

There were always voices within her, which pinged and spoke to her, and led her along a path that she herself did not often understand. However, before the voice could resurface and remind her about the laptop that she had to invest in, she was at the counter, charging the book on her credit card.

She would worry about the credit card and other bills later, she thought to herself, as she reached her apartment. She quickly changed her clothes and got into pyjamas and a t-shirt, slouched into her favourite chair by the window and opened the book to enter its pages, as if it were a large room that had to be explored.

She loved the smell of anticipation in a new book. Just as she liked the musty, dusty smell of learning and knowledge in libraries and the overwhelming sensation of seeing row upon row of books in the endless racks of a library. She held the book to her face, wanting to savour the mysterious attraction of the writer.

Tamaara liked it that this book, small and compact as it was, was untouched by anyone else. (She had made sure the shop assistant brought her a copy that was shrink-wrapped. As if she didn't want its fragrances to be dissipated in the air around the store). She ran her fingers over the typeface, caressing the lines and the spaces between them.

And once more, she looked at the face on the inside of the jacket. Who was he, she asked herself aloud, switching off the cacophony of the television which was often a background to the silence of her life.

So here were the first few sentences, she thought, as she sunk into the book: 'What was the charivari in this quaint French town that Anna was becoming a part of, when all that she was doing was to stand on the street and watch?'

'Charivari', what a lovely word, she stopped to muse, as she rolled the word around on her tongue.

Tamaara was yet to Google the word, but for the moment she

was happy to be saying it aloud. As the French would say it. As she read the book, she felt the same overpowering of the senses as when she had dabbed a bit of *mogra* fragrance on her wrists once.

The story was of a Sri Lankan priest, who was pleading with a Christian god to save him from the memory of the woman he had fallen in love with. Tamaara loved it that he kept referring to the memory of the woman's feet, which he could not get out of his mind.

She must go for a pedicure one of these days, she told herself, getting up to see what was in the fridge that she could now nibble. Maybe she could have those dark and bitter chocolates, which she consumed by the slab because they flooded her with the warm feeling of being loved.

Unwrapping the chocolate, she wondered what it would be like to meet the writer who wrote so beautifully.

She was a dreamer and was often told, "Tamaara, you live in another world that is not real at all."

What is reality, she mused. Certainly not editing an in-house magazine that was full of photographs of the hotel's celebrity guests. Or worse, had odd recipes of Burmese noodles and Phad Thai Curry by the chefs that she was not sure who was going to try out. If she ever married, and could afford not to work, she would be happy not proof reading a magazine that was called, of all the things, 'A La Carte'!

A few chapters into the book, she decided to shift to her bedroom so that she could lie in the bed and read. And when she switched the lights off, she began to think of Arawinda.

Would she ever meet a man like Arawinda who had such a way with words? And what would happen to her if she met him, would they exchange words and sentences as other couples exchanged bits of gossip or everyday news of their school going children?

Maybe she would cook him those string-hoppers that Sri Lankans loved, and some mutton stew. Even if she herself had turned into a vegetarian after accidentally walking into the kitchen of the hotel to see a chicken being wrung to death.

Or she could sit by his side (in her imagination she was not sure as yet what clothes she would wear, the mauve sari or the *kantha*-worked *dupatta* in blue and green and other colours) and hand him pens, or clean his laptop on and off, or why, even help him look for a word in the dictionary.

However, what if he was one of those writers like Poe or Twain, about whom there were dreadful stories that they locked themselves in rooms or stood continuously while writing. Well, she would figure all that out if she ever met Arawinda, the man with the piercing eyes.

A few days later, at the office, she was surprised when her boss (oh, why couldn't she have a male boss, they were less contentious) announced that the publishing company wanted to launch the book by the Sri Lankan writer Arawinda Sena at their hotel, and could she be a darling and get the media and a few society women for the event?

"I've never heard of the writer, Taa-m-aara, have you?" Mythili asked. Mythili could never say her name correctly even after a year, but she let it pass.

"Mythili…" she was about to launch into a narration of how she had been to the bookstore only a few days ago and bought the hardback edition, when Mythili lost interest in the conversation and retreated to answer another of those calls she got all the time on her BlackBerry. To Tamaara, anyone who carried a BlackBerry had important things to do in life. She herself did not have one.

"God, why do I even attempt to have a conversation with Mythili!" Tamaara muttered to herself. But what luck that Arawinda should be coming to Delhi. She would go to the airport to pick him up. And Mythili had told her there would be a dinner for him with a few guests from Delhi's literary set.

She was not sure if she should wear her silk *salwar-kurta* or her linen pants. Or maybe even go and buy something more stylish like a silk skirt, and an expensive scarf. She wanted to look 'with it', as if she met writers like him every day. The last one she had met was Vikram Roy who often came to their hotel for a drink. All that he did, however, was to say a polite hello to her when she had asked to be introduced to him.

Tamaara was determined to look her best when she met Arawinda, not just at the book launch but even when he would be introduced to all of them that evening.

She must not only finish reading the book tonight, but see if she could go to the spa sometime and have a facial that was guaranteed to make her face glow, or so the advertisements promised poor unsuspecting women like herself.

If nothing else, she would at least soak her feet in a tub of hot water at home and scrub them and paint her nails so that he would notice her feet, if not her face and her presence. Not Mythili's, she hoped. She had to admit, Mythili not only had beautiful feet but lovely pairs of sandals, and looked chic all the time – with colourful, beaded necklaces around her neck and large *bindis* on her forehead.

"Hello ma'am," he said in his deep voice. A bit like Lawrence Olivier, she mused. "Are you also a Shakespearean actor?" she said, only to realize that there had been no sound from her throat, and he had moved on to say something to Mythili, who was telling him what she thought about his book.

Until yesterday she had not even known he was a writer, and what was she saying now that he found so profound, Tamaara wondered.

And then, suddenly, everyone was looking at her and she became flustered. Had her *dupatta* fallen off her shoulder or had she simply forgotten to wear her sandals?

Arawinda was actually saying something to her. "If it's not too much trouble, I would love to see Delhi in the morning, with this young lady," he said, which she faintly registered in the recesses of her mind.

It was almost as if there were two people within her now. One that was responding to Arawinda and her colleagues, and the other that was saying to herself, 'Oh, no, what am I going to do with him the whole day? What if he asks me the meanings of words, like *charivari*?' Or asks me what I thought of Sri Lankan writers?

Should she read the book again or Google him, so that she would be able to say something sensible to him? Do writers expect you to have read their books? She wanted to sound like a bright and a well-read woman, not one of those dull PR persons who spoke a lot about nothing.

She could barely sleep that night because of excitement. And even before she was fully awake the next morning, she heard someone knocking on her door. She was surprised to see, but didn't let it show on her face, that it was the famous writer himself!

She was under the impression that it was she who was supposed to pick him up from the hotel, and here he was at her door. Had he asked the driver to bring him to the house, she was not sure, but he was saying, "What a lovely Indian morning. May I come in?"

He left his slippers outside the door (she certainly liked these courtesies that Sri Lankans followed much like Indians) and walked into her apartment. She had forgotten to put away her copy of

Faith, so it lay there open on her favourite pages, which she had been re-reading in the night, not because she was going to meet him, but more because she was fascinated with way he wrote: 'Words seduce. Anna knew that as she listened to the priest evoke his boyhood in Ireland through sentences and landscapes.'

So that he didn't see the mess of her rooms, she steered him into the little sit-out in the verandah that had the nicest view of the adjacent gardens.

"Do you drink tea, young lady?" She was going to open her mouth to say something, when he asked, "May I call you Tamaara? Does it mean lotus in Indian languages too?" he asked, making himself comfortable in the cane chair. One of its legs was broken and had been fixed temporarily. She hoped it wouldn't give way at the precise hour a famous writer had come to her small apartment.

If there was a moment that she would hold forever in her memory, it would be this – the easy familiarity between them, as if he came home to have tea and toast with her every morning, maybe after a walk in Lodhi or some other garden. That memorable gesture of lifting a cup to sip and looking at her, waiting to continue a conversation they might have left incomplete a day ago.

She excused herself to get ready. She was a little worried that he was going to follow her into her room, but he did not.

When she emerged after a few minutes, he moved closer to look at her and smiled, lifting his hand to wipe the black of the eyeliner that had smudged her face. She wanted to ask, do I look Ok, are these clothes alright? But she didn't, and neither did he say anything. There was a moment of pause.

"May I choose the footwear?" he asked, surveying the rows of shoes and slippers in the small cane rack she kept in the foyer of her apartment.

He didn't wait for her opinion, and picked out a pair of dark brown sandals. They were tight, one size too small, but when someone she admired was asking her to wear them she was not going to get into lengthy explanations of how she had bought them without first trying them on and of how she thought they were a steal at that time. They were anyway going around in a car, and hopefully she wouldn't have to walk much.

She pulled the apartment door shut behind her, and both of them got into the car. She turned to him to ask what he would like to see in Delhi. The Qutb Minar or Red Fort?

"I will go wherever you take me, Tamaara," he said leaning back in the seat and closing his eyes.

For a second, she wanted to run a finger along his face. Especially on the scar, which gave his face its ruffian-like character. She could not imagine his face without that defining line from the mouth to his eye.

When he opened his eyes, he caught her staring at him and knew she was going to ask him about his scar. "It's a long story, suffice it to say it's been part of me since I was a boy," he said.

He did not show any surprise or probably was not listening when she told the driver to take them to National Gallery of Modern Art first.

She wanted to show him the works of Amrita Sher-Gil, a painter she admired greatly for the rebel she was. "Have you heard of her?" she inquired, walking past him to buy the entry tickets. "No, not her, and until yesterday I didn't know you either. Does it matter now?"

Was he saying all this to fluster her? She did not know, and in what seemed like a natural gesture their hands sometimes touched, or their shoulders, while looking at the paintings and then walking around the museum.

"Do you want to go to the hotel to eat? I think Mythili is expecting you for lunch," she said seeing that it was nearing afternoon.

"No, let's go to Old Delhi and see what we can have," he said, guiding her towards the car. "Everything in this country has so much character. Even this Ambassador car," he said smiling at Ram Singh, the driver, who had by now begun to wonder who this celebrity was, as he had driven the likes of Richard Gere around Delhi many times.

In Chandni Chowk, they ate *aloo paranthas* made fresh and hot, and the plate of *gulab jamoons* he insisted on sharing with her. When some of the *jamoon* syrup dripped on her face as she was eating one, he took out his handkerchief to wipe it off.

Embarrassed, she wanted to ask him who he was, who so fascinated her. "Who are you?" she asked frowning, both from the heat and the excess food.

"Arawinda at your service, ma'am," he said, wiping his hands on his *kurta*.

"Are you going to wear a *kurta* for the book reading too this evening?" she asked, to divert his mind (and hers) from what, to her, was such an intimate moment.

"Why, what do you want me to wear?" he asked. "Anything," she said, wondering why he wanted her opinion. "And, can you wear a sari? I like Indian women in saris," he said.

The book reading went off well, and there were reports in the newspapers of what a charming writer Arawinda was. There were interviews with him on all the channels.

All that she remembered of the evening was that she slept by his side later that night, and not as on previous nights with his book.

She felt sad when he left the next morning. And she could not even talk with anyone else about this fleeting romance. Who would believe her, or her impetuosity or the madness?

But then, love was a matter of insanity. He had said that too in his book.

BOA MAMA, WHO WILL SING YOUR SONGS?

BOA MAMA WANTED to lie down. She began to walk towards her coconut tree by the sea. The tree had been her favourite since she was that high. When she came to the tree she lay down and let the evening sun wash over her body. Over her nipples and navel. She felt comforted by the smell of the earth. This was the earth where everyone she loved was buried.

Her mother, who had taught her the Aka Bo songs of the Andamans; her sisters, who had been born in the same mud hut as her; the man with a front tooth missing whom she had been intimate with.

Every one, everyone was gone.

She rubbed her sagging and tired body against the roughness of a tree, whose roots too were buried in the earth, thinking of the daughters she had not borne. And she wailed over the emptiness of her womb, and for her loneliness. Even the distant roar of her beloved ocean could not silence that sorrow.

Like other girls of her tribe, she had learnt to fish, to hunt for pigs, and to weave baskets. She had learnt to dig for potatoes.

But what she had loved the most was learning the Aka Bo songs from her mother. On evenings such as this one, her mother would braid her curly hair, singing as she wove her daughter's hair, over and under, this way and that. Boa Mama would join her in her sweet little voice.

Boa Mama sang now, lying on the earth, her voice quavering and rasping, listening to her mother's voice in the song, and her mother's mother before that, as the light of night gathered around her.

Boa Mama could not see all that well in the dark. She didn't eat very much either, not even her favourite fish that her man used to get for her until some years ago.

At the hospital, they had put her through machines, and told her she was sick from old age. She had laughed and told herself, "I know my time is coming. I want to go. I want to be buried in this earth where mama is, where my sisters are and where my grandmamma is", and she sang a song, in her grief. The birds on the trees nearby twittered unaware of Mama's grief.

What Boa Mama had not lost was her ability to walk the great distances of the jungle, and find her tree. And what she was never unlikely to lose was her voice.

At one time, when she sang just the way her mamma had taught her, a woman here, a child there, and a man from deep inside the jungle would join in the chorus and the song would rise and rise like the waves of the ocean, until there was only the crescendo.

Now there was only silence, a silence which had seeped and run into her body. But she opened her heart and sang so loud that the earth parted. Like it did when the tsunami lashed the islands many moons ago.

Sometime in the night, Mama went to sleep. After 85 years. There was no one to mourn her passing. No one to take turns to sit by her body and sing the Aka Bo songs of mourning, until her soul left her body on the tenth day.

Boa Mama will never again walk in the jungle or by the sea. Nor sing an Aka Bo Song. Her mother will not sing. Her daughters will not sing.

Mama, wake up. Wake up and sing your songs.

(This short story was written when Boa Mama, the last surviving member of the Aka Bo tribe in Andamans, died at the age of 85.)

ONE OF A KIND

SHE PULLED THE comfortable rocking chair to a corner near the edge of the verandah so that she was closer to the *raat ki rani* shrub that threw a faint light as well as spread an aroma at this time of night. It was late, and she sat closetted in the silence of darkness. A cricket chirped hysterically, and a frog leapt on the wet lawn.

She had been sitting there, waiting for he granddaughter Raasi, who had gone to watch a film with Rohit, the young boy who dropped in so often. At least, they were open about their relationship and love, she thought with satisfaction.

But then, who does not want to know the love of a man, she asked herself.

Even *she* had known love and passion. And pain. And it had not been Raasi's grandfather, good man that he was, with whom she had shared an interesting life of dinner parties, transfers, constant packing, setting up home, and bringing up children. He had been a judge at the district courts and there was no doubt they made a grand couple when they made an entrance at a gathering. He so tall and distinguished in his silk *bandhgalas* and she in her brightly coloured Kanchi saris and red ruby earrings.

She had not even turned 40 when Amitabh died one morning of a heart attack, leaving her with two young children. Only she knew how young. She, along with the boys, had sat huddled under the staircase one night, wondering what to do with the rest of her life. There were so many things to do, so many bank accounts and papers to be sorted out that she did not even have the luxury of mourning her husband's passing.

Besides, she had to worry about finding a job, and teaching English literature was all that she could do, so when the local college offered her a position only because her husband had laid its foundation stone, she took it up.

She couldn't be choosy now, she told herself. Her parents wanted her to come back to Hyderabad. "We will be there for you," her mother had urged her at the time of the funeral.

But she had been stubborn about not wanting to move to another city. She would have had to give up the rambling old bungalow with ancient trees, which had been their official residence in Agra, but the city had other smaller houses that she could afford to move into.

She had quit her job as a lecturer after the children were born, and with all those postings in small towns, she had never really looked for a job. But the college in Delhi where she was working before she got married, had kept her place vacant for a long time hoping she would return.

"What is the need to work, Rani?" Amitabh had said. Her name was Naina, but everyone had called her Rani, a name her doting father had given and stuck to her for life. "Enjoy your time with the boys, both of us know how fast children grow. Travel with me, see new places. Even if I know we will have to carry a trunk full of your books," Amitabh had said.

He thought she spent far too much time reading, and would distract her by saying something like, "Why don't you make that *palak dal* for my lunch tomorrow? The Andhra *dal* you said you learnt from your grandmother in Hyderabad?"

Tomorrow is another day, she would want to respond, feeling like Scarlett O'Hara. But she would sigh, kiss him on the cheek, and say, "Okay then, *palakura pappu* and rice for lunch tomorrow." She was pleased that at least, he didn't always ask for *masala dosa* and *sambar* which most north Indians associated south Indian cooking with.

She looked at her slender wrist, wanting to see how late Raasi was, forgetting momentarily that she had long ago given up wearing a watch.

After Amitabh passed away, she had stopped feeling the need to mark the passing of the hours. This may not have been entirely in mourning, but rather a rebellion against Amitabh's obsessive need to be punctual – his need to look at the clock so that he would get into the car exactly at 9:45 am and reach his office by 10:15, and still have 15 minutes to have a cup of tea by himself, before visitors and work started pouring in.

Who knows the cause of our internal rebellions, whether it rises from an innocuous thought that is planted when we are least aware of it? In some such manner, what we call 'character' emerges.

Like Avinash's need to carry a wad of hundred rupee notes in his wallet. "That's for all those years in college when I didn't have money, Naina. When, I ate one meal a day so that I could still go see a Truffaut film, buy a Hemingway or a *Paris Review*," he had said.

"If you ever need money, you know whom to ask," he would say sitting at her feet. "I adore you Naina, you know that," he would remark with earnestness.

He was obsessed with collecting trivial bits of knowledge, just the way someone collects paintings or jewellery. His mind was filled with all sorts of information, which he wanted to share with her; in the car, at home, anywhere.

"Do you know the first novel to have ever been written on a typewriter, Naina?" he had once asked. With her kind of memory, even if she knew which one it was she couldn't tell him. He patted her hand, and said, "*Tom Sawyer*, Prof."

And once, after making love, he had asked her, "Do you know the first couple to be shown in bed together on television?" "No, I don't know," she had said, not really caring if she knew the answer to that one either. "Fred and Wilma of *Flintstones*," he had said, pulling her ears.

He was good looking in a healthy sort of way, though she wished he would stop wearing a crumpled cotton *kurta* whenever he came to see her. And his hair was always in a mess. But she liked that. It added to his boyish charm.

Sometimes, he seemed only that much older than her two boys, she would think, as she ran her fingers through his mop of hair and whispered, "I love you so much, Avinash."

She sighed wondering where Raasi was, looking anxiously towards the wicker gate. She stretched her legs, thinking they hurt so much these days. "Can I press your feet, should I rub your back?" he would ask anxiously, always wanting to do something for her.

He would take her to the movies, in his newly-acquired Premier Padmini. He would get her a big bag of popcorn, which they would munch together. He was a chain smoker, and though many times she had tried to make him quit, she never really succeeded. She smiled to herself as she thought of all the times they had spent in his three-bedroom home, which was quite a fancy house for one so young; but then he had just got his first promotion. It was a foreign bank, so he felt rich all the time.

Other men gave flowers and perfumes to those they loved. Or diamonds. But the first gift he ever gave her was a small notebook that he had brought back from a trip to Bombay. It was made by a company called 'One Of A Kind'.

He had been so excited about his discovery that he had called her from there, wanting to know if he could get her a gift.

"Special. Just like you," he said, when he had slipped the tiny yellow book into her hand.

"So that you can write your poems and stories in them".

"I've stopped writing you know. Didn't feel like after Amitabh..." she told him, realizing immediately that she might have hurt him by her abruptness.

"I want you to," he said firmly, scribbling in the book, 'Just like my love, one of a kind'.

He then brought out a bottle of wine, chilled just as she liked it, and put on his favourite Beethoven Symphony. Though she liked music, any music, she really didn't understand Beethoven, or Brahms or Chopin. So, instead, she walked around the house wanting to organize the books on his shelf, just as she would have in her sons' hostel rooms, but she let it be. He had already asked her once why she mothered him so.

Revathi, her daughter-in-law, opened the door to see what she was doing. "Amma, all by yourself? Shall I get you something? Your shawl, a cup of hot cocoa?"

She was a good woman, Rajiv's wife. Good-looking as well. She hoped there was passion in their marriage. What was a marriage without love and companionship, finally?

Or what was life without love, she had often asked on those lonely evenings when she only had her two boys for company. To have someone to sit with in the evenings, and watch the moon rise, or to have coffee in the mornings and share gossip.

She had done that with Amitabh on many a morning, when he was not on the phone discussing a case or immersed in the politics of the town. He had his tea of course, and she her coffee, but at least they both had liked two spoonfuls of sugar in their cup.

They would sit like that sipping tea or coffee, and share the gossip about the neighbours – of how someone's mother-in-law was visiting the family, or of how a driver had run away with a maid. The usual gossip that wives shared with their husbands, who were otherwise preoccupied. Yes, she missed that the most. That she did not have someone to wake up with, soak in the morning sun, and watch another day take over their life.

But as someone had written to her in one of the many condolence letters that came her way throughout the first year after Amitabh's passing, you have to learn to play with the cards you are dealt with. She certainly had learnt to play without the ace of hearts.

And more than anything she understood the quietness that crept through the walls of the house, into her bones. When she could see the word 'loneliness' take shape in front of her. Like that, take the shape of a huge monster, so scary that she no longer worried about nightmares.

"I will hold you in my arms when you sleep. I will stay awake and watch you through the night," he had said. And knowing how afraid she was of accidents and sudden deaths, he had held her close to say, "And yes, I will be there if you were ever to die before me. I will not let that happen, no, never," he had said.

She wondered if his ardour was because he was so young. Would the world make him cynical soon enough? She could not understand why he loved her in this way, and with such passion.

"I will do anything for you, Naina," he said. He loved to call her Naina, and not like everyone else, Rani.

"Shall I jump off the wall?" he had asked her once, when she challenged his passion.

She feared the impulsiveness of his youth. But his passion made her feel that she was still a woman. And not just Naina, mother of two boys now in colleges away from home, or an English professor. Being in love with him was a way of feeling she was alive. Like pinching herself, and feeling the hurt, making sure she was not dead as yet.

And how did she come to feel any love for him? This young man, who had impressed her the very first evening they met, when he had offered to drop her home?

On a dark night, just like this one. Had it been his sense of optimism? Of how he succeeded in dragging her out of the chair to waltz with her? Indeed, now she knew, he had dragged a woman back to life, and life back into a woman.

"Yes Revathi, can you bring my shawl. I am feeling cold," she told her daughter-in-law. "And why hasn't Raasi come back as yet? It's so late," she murmured.

Many times, she had wanted to ask him, "Do you know how old I am?" Or how old her children were. But she had never hidden any of those things from him. "Is it menopause, all these mood swings?" he would ask her innocently. At least he knew what menopause was, she thought relieved that he could handle her being older.

She had been shy about showing him her ageing body, but in the passion with which he touched her, her body could have had no faults. Not even the flab that was creeping around her waist. Those days she had wished she had perfect curves, and a 14-inch waist like her favourite movie character, Scarlett.

Scarlett was a fictional heroine, she thought, breaking her reverie. But here was Raasi who was the most gorgeous 18-year-old she had seen in her life.

Raasi would not dress up, however much she scolded her. But that was the arrogance of the young, who never imagined that all this would wane, and one day all that you could offer the man you loved was your kindness and generosity. And your aching arms, which wanted to embrace someone, anyone, so badly. Was that why, when he had walked into her heart, she had not even murmured in protest? She ought to have, really, to prevent the devastation that followed.

But she had protested the first time he had called her, a call that came when she was on her way to college, to say that he loved her. Immensely, he said, and she hurried back to her room to look at herself in the mirror and see the woman that Avinash was in love with.

She had even stopped wearing all those beautiful saris she had worn in an earlier lifetime. The embroidered blouses that she had worn in college. She redid the kohl in her eyes, and wore her deep red ruby earrings again. Now that someone was in love with her, she felt responsible for the way she looked.

But why did he love her, a woman in her fifties? She had been beautiful, yes, once, but not now with all that grey in her hair, which she never camouflaged.

She looked like someone to whom a young man came for

blessings, touching her feet in respect, rather than someone who would tickle her feet with passion. But how old was he? So much younger than her, maybe a decade at least? He must have been in his early forties, she had once surmised never caring to ask his age now that they were in love.

"No Avinash, you do not love me. You love the idea of an older woman in your life," she had said, pushing him away from her.

She could have, of course, not taken his calls, and not encouraged all of this. But where was the choice when you had a storm coming towards you? She could have either lain low and let it pass. Or, she could have opened her arms and embraced it. And be embraced in return.

When they were away from each other, they became different people – obsessive lovers that you read about in books. Or watch in movies, thinking, how can a woman become so obsessed with another human being? Or he would lie awake, unable to sleep, wanting to be with her. They were two insane people, in the city of love, Agra.

Avinash, who was romantic otherwise, had his own theories about the Taj, having grown up in its shadow. "Look Naina, that was a man obsessed with himself and his ideas of grandeur. A marble mausoleum? How cold for his lady love to be buried in!" he had once argued during a long drive after which they had sat by the Yamuna.

"No mausoleums for my Naina. We will die together and be buried together," he had said, taking her hand. "Has anyone loved you the way I have?"

No one had loved her the way he did. No one would. Why had she let go of him then? The day that he had asked her to marry him, she had refused.

And he simply got up and walked out of her life.

She had wanted to call, talk to him and explain. That, she was at the end of her life. A few more years, and she would not even have this health. That he was at the threshold of his life, and ought to marry someone younger.

She heard the car, and Raasi opening the gate to come in with her boyfriend. "*Daadi*, you're still here?" the young girl asked, giving her a hug.

"I was waiting for you, my love," she said getting up to go inside.

"*Daadi*, I have to take you to the hospital tomorrow. Wake me up at 8, please," Raasi said, leaving a trail of happiness and youth behind her.

She could still feel the tears in his eyes as he had whispered to her on the banks of Yamuna, "Naina, no one will ever love you the way I do."

No one has, Avinash, she thought, switching off the lights in her room. There was this four-poster bed now. And the memory of Avinash, who had said he would hold her when she lay dying.

She would ask Raasi tomorrow to look for his phone number among her diaries and books.

WE WERE YOUNG ONCE

FOREVER THE ROAR of the ocean in my ears, over and above everything else. That sound is like a heartbeat, a constant backdrop to the drama of my life, which has been a comedy surely. Sometimes, the ocean is more overbearing than naughty children on the street, but on dark moonless nights, she is silent, like a satiated lover.

I am from what is a small island, Diu, where I grew up playing football and other games in its narrow streets, saluting the Portuguese officers who winked at us – young and recalcitrant as we were – while walking around the town. No one played cricket; that game was popular in British India (which we were not part of). In places like Poona and Bombay.

I remember the loud gong of the bell in the centre of the town. It would boom three times a day.

Where were all the cheap watches you can buy now, imported from China or some such place? In those days, only the rich could afford to buy clocks and watches, which were expensive because they were handcrafted in Lisbon.

The rest of us marked the passing of the hour by the sound of the bell in the city centre, which was especially loud at four in the evening, when the local factory workers and servants wound up their jobs to return home. My friends and I would sometimes stand below the tower house, where the bell hung, and feel its vibrations reverberate through our bodies. The Portuguese officers who rang them were that strong, from all the mutton they ate, no doubt.

But that was a long time ago.

These days, I need help even to cross the street on which I had once played football and *kabaddi*. But look at the traffic now, so many cars on the roads that were once meant for horse carriages and the lovely Ford cars.

I will let you in on a secret, though it might seem that I am boasting. I was one of the first to own a car in this town. A Morris Minor, which I would clean myself and drive around, every morning I would ask my wife – who was far nicer looking in those days than she is now – to come along for a drive. She never wanted to come in the mornings. She had the cooking to do, and the children to take care of.

But in the evenings, she would wear colourful *bandhini* saris and shyly get into the car with me. It was not easy for us to go out together, for the whole town would have been amused at such a display of our romance and would have teased me no end. This is a small town, so there was not very far we could go.

But we were quite a sight, going around the town like the king and queen of Portugal. Sometimes, Nirmala, that's her name, would even move closer to me while I was driving. "Careful," she would say touching me on my shoulder. "Don't drive so fast." I used to like the sound of the bangles she wore. Plenty of glass bangles. I was just a small-town doctor, what else could I buy her?

Have I told you how I met Nirmala? Though her family and mine had houses next to each other and we almost shared the same wall (yes, the houses are that close in this town they still are), yet I had never met her formally during my entire childhood. Strangely. I guess girls then were far too shy to come out. Or maybe I was the shy young boy.

But very soon, she had gone off to Mozambique with her parents. They had a small shop there. Selling *dal* and rice. My parents too had migrated to Mozambique as petty traders, then finally opening a jewellery shop. Our parents had agreed to the marriage there and she was sent off to Diu, where we got married in a simple Hindu ceremony.

There is very little hair left on my head. My feet are swollen. But the hands, the hands are fine. I can still hold the torch and throw light on someone's tonsils to see if it's infected in there. They don't make those sturdy steel torches anymore, just small ones in plastic, in red and green. My son uses one of those.

Did I tell you he is an Ayurvedic physician? I wanted him to be a doctor. He didn't make it to the medical college, so he went down to Trivandrum to study Ayurveda. But he is not beyond prescribing a Crocin or Lopomid to his patients who want to recover quickly.

People don't want to be sick anymore. They all just want to be in good health, and what for do you think? To go to the cinema and restaurants! Illness is a pause in life, a comma in a sentence that allows you to stop and catch your breath. But who would listen to such wisdom from an old doctor like me?

I am only a GP, with no fancy degrees. These days, unless you have a string of degrees after your name, no one will even come to you for treatment. Do they come to see the doctor or to examine his degrees, I sometimes wonder. And what do these doctors with degrees do? They cannot even diagnose a simple fever without asking the patient to get an X-ray or a CT scan. Who talks of a simple physical examination of a patient, or, for that matter, who will pay you a consultation fee if you just examined the patient, gave him a paracetamol and sent him home?

Have I told you all these things already? You will have to forgive me if I am rambling. As I said, I am getting on in years and there is a rush of memories. These memories are like the meteors that leave a trail of light behind them. My life is behind me now. At 80, your life and memories are the only things trailing behind you.

Yes, I am a man prone to using metaphors. I did rather well in English and Portuguese literature in high school. Read all the great dramas and stories. If I had not wanted to become a doctor, I would certainly have got into a theatre company and travelled all over.

Now they have more of Gujarati theatre, but in my youth, we saw so many great plays – in Portuguese. I can still read Portuguese, and my son is often amused when Nirmala and I speak in Portuguese, when we don't want him to understand what we are saying.

Now, the Portuguese were something else though, I have nothing against the present governments, the BJP or the Congress, who took over after what they called the 'Liberation'. But the Portuguese government was meticulous with their record-keeping, and kept the town spick and span. A sanitary inspector would go around the town in the morning and the evening. It's hard to believe, but we even needed a travel permit when we had to go to the cities in British India.

Back then, in Diu, we were more familiar with Portuguese culture than Indian. Like many Gujaratis then, my family too migrated not to Lisbon, but to Portuguese Africa – Mozambique.

They took my sister with them, but left me behind with my grandparents. Sadly, they had no particular plan for my life. *Nana*, who was a small time accountant in the village, had no time for me. *Nani* was good to me, although not of much help when I wanted to choose a career.

I saw the village *vaid* and decided I too wanted to give medicines and make people feel better. I liked the way he was invited everywhere and made to feel special at family get-togethers. And more than that, when the neigbouring *kaaki* was unwell and grinding her teeth with stomach ache, it was he, by his touch and with herbs, who made her feel better so that she began to smile. I didn't like to see her crying like that.

Not just she, but anyone. I thought if this *vaid* died who would make the sick people feel better? I was determined to study hard and get a medical degree and come back to Diu to be a doctor.

I moved to Panjim in Goa, which was where the medical college was. My father thought I should go to Mozambique and help him there with his businesses.

"Why do you want to study medicine? We need you here, come and help us in the businesses," he wrote to me, one angry letter after another.

But this man, my father, I did not meet him many times. He didn't want to leave his business and come to his village, and I did not want to go there because I didn't want to do all the things they did. I didn't want to be uneducated like my father, shouting even at the people who helped him with the shop. I wanted to be kind to people.

I have a bad cough these days. My son wants to take me to a big hospital in Bombay. But why would I want to go there? What are they going to tell an 80-year-old man, anyway? That I should stop smoking? That I should cut down on *ghee* and sweets? That I do not have many days to live? It's not how many more days that are left that matter anymore, but how well you have lived life.

I relive each day in my memory, savouring it like those chocolates my wife will let me have once in a while. Sometimes... I live my life again, recalling the fragrance of my wife's body, which smelt of Yardley powder, or the sound of a *Raag Bhairavi* I heard once on someone else's transistor radio, around which we had gathered, and wondered if Pandit Bhimsen Joshi himself was sitting inside and singing.

My son said they think it's a cancer of the lungs. Nirmala says with all those cigarettes I smoked through college, what else would I get? Not the Padma Shri certainly.

Though she will not say it she feels sorry for me, I know, when I sit up in the nights, unable to breathe. Every time my son takes me to the hospital, all that I want to do is come home. I really should have been kinder to all my patients who protested when I told them they should move closer to a big hospital in case of an emergency. They wanted to remain in their homes. There comes a moment when you don't want to fight for your life anymore.

Let me tell you about my medical college. My father refused to send money for my education. It was my grandmother who pawned her nose ring and pearl earrings to give me money to pay for some of the fees.

In Panjim, I worked in the house of a well-off family, the Shahs. They were from our town and knew us. Those days, of course, all of us knew everyone else, so this man was like a *maama* to me.

I didn't know much housework, but helped *maama* in the garden, and *maami* in the kitchen. She made the most delicious food. On the days I went to their house, she fed me the fancy Gujarati food. All sorts of *farsans* and *jalebis*. Especially *khandvi*, which I liked so much.

They had a daughter, who was a little younger than me. Neela, they called her. But her real name was Neelakshi. She had beautiful eyes, an even finer nose, and dark long hair that she tied with ribbons. I even remember the colour of those ribbons – orange and white – quite indistinguishable from the marigolds and jasmines she would tuck into her long plait.

"Neela," her mother would call for her to come into the kitchen and help her peel the potatoes, or to reach for a pickle jar that was kept too high on the shelf. I would put a stool for Neelakshi, who would daintily lift the *ghagra* she was wearing, which reached just above her ankles, and hold my hand to climb on the stool. She would then place her hand on my shoulder, before she jumped down to run out of the kitchen.

"Neela!" her mother would cry with exasperation, but Neela would be gone. She moved like lightning against a dark sky. Illuminating everything with her quick movements.

I have seen beautiful things in my life. A *bulbul* preening itself on rain-drenched mornings. A shaft of morning light streaming into the courtyard. Was beauty within a thing itself or was it in the mystery that the thing left behind? When light entered the courtyard like that in the Shah's house in Goa, I would think of Guru Dutt films. That play of light on his favourite heroine, Waheeda. Now that was beauty that needed no embellishment. Like my Neela.

Did I say *my* Neela? She was never mine. Or maybe she always was. Was I not the one who busied myself during her wedding, putting the coconuts in the packets and welcoming the guests, taking them upstairs to the dining hall and telling them politely,

"Aunty, you must not go without eating. Without showering your blessings on our Neela."

And Neela, how fine she looked in her *gharchola* with gold threads woven into a chequered pattern. *Maami* had sent me (and no one else) to the tailor to get the matching blouse, just one day before the wedding day. And with her long hair braided into one long plait, interspersed with jasmines and roses. I was the one who went to the market to order the flowers for Neela.

"Where are you, *beta*?" *maami*'s plaintive cry still sounds in my ears.

"Don't you know the day for the wedding is fast approaching and we have done practically nothing?" She sounded so helpless that even before the classes were over, I was at their doorstep by mid-afternoon on those long summer days.

Nirmala is tapping me on the shoulder and telling me not to think so much. She says I have not slept for two whole nights. I should humour her. She has been a good wife. Even now it is she who cleans me, wipes the dribble that constantly oozes from my mouth. I will pretend to sleep. I can always close my eyes, even if sleep eludes me these days.

Ah, what is that? Is that a shaft of light streaming through that window? Why, is Neelakshi calling me?

Such fierceness in the sound of the sea tonight. Ah, it must be a full moon night.

There is only the pain wreaking havoc in my body. The pain that made my patients cry for another dose of morphine, that I prescribed without emotion, not realizing what pain could be.

My Neela, why does she not appear before me? Where is death? I wish she would embrace me now.

MY NAME IS MEENAKSHI

SHE WAS TIRED of the television serials they aired these days, the ones with women who wept over every little thing. She flipped channels hoping to watch a good film.

Her favourite among the current crop of movie stars was Brad Pitt – also her granddaughter's favourite. She seemed to love buying posters of him and CDs of his films. He was a nice-looking boy alright, American she imagined, but was certainly no match for her very own favourite, Gregory Peck. Women of her generation felt that the Hindi film star Dev Anand looked like him, but for her, there was no one like the original.

There was not a film of his that she would miss, though her family was shocked that she could watch *Guns of Navarone* so many times. And how she had cut classes at Stella Maris to see his films, only she and her friends knew. The Mother Superior never did get wind of it, thankfully. Nor her father, who would have thrashed her if he had as much as smelt a whiff of the fact that she, a well brought-up girl from a conservative Brahmin family, was seen outside the college premises. Even words like 'premises' had become so old fashioned now, she sighed to herself. It was no great act of rebellion if her granddaughter or her friends cut a few classes for movies these days.

"Amma!" the cook was calling loudly from the kitchen, above the noise of the hissing pressure cooker.

Amma? Was that what she had become over the decades? She had had a name once, but that was so long ago that she had got used to being known simply as Amma to everyone. This included her two children, Jo and Jan (when they went to study in America the two had anglicized their lovely names Jyotsna and Janardan to Jo and Jan).

Even their friends, who were all grown up and working now, addressed her as "Amma" and touched her feet. Why, even the neighbour's newly arrived daughter-in-law, Raji, began to call her "Amma". She was a nice girl who came from Bombay and lent her Agatha Christie mysteries from her collection, which she was re-reading now.

The cook, the maid, the flower man, even the *thottakaran* Arumugam, who had recently joined the household staff, called her "Amma". He slept most of the time under the shadow of the mango tree or pretended to bustle about, digging the garden. But these days, she felt detached from the running of the house. It was after all her daughter's home and responsibility, and she was not going to worry if there was no *pulungula arasi* for *dosas* or if the garden began to look like the Mudumalai jungle.

"Amma, there is no *karvepalai* in the fridge. Should I send the driver to get some?" the cook was asking her.

Amma turned the television volume down to ask, "What

Ramaniamma, can you not make *rasam* without the *karvepalai*? And, anyway, what were you doing when we sent Mani yesterday to the market to get vegetables?"

These days Amma was getting tired of the cook asking her all sorts of things. First, she had become the universal mother, and then everyone was asking her advice about this or that. Just the other day Raji was asking her how to draw *kolams* in the front yard of the house.

Another of Jo's friends actually came with a recipe book to ask her how to make *rasam* just like hers, with its aroma wafting around the house and into the neighbours'. She didn't like to cook that much these days, but she had to get into the kitchen when Ramaniamma didn't turn up one evening and Jo was bringing her colleague home for dinner. Anyway, how do you teach someone to make good *rasam*? You just throw in a tomato, the *rasam* powder and some *karvepalai*. What is a 'pinch' of salt that they wrote of in cookbooks? How could she explain to the girl that you needed good *perungayam* to make *rasam*?

Oh, who was that, peering in through the window? It looked like it was Arumugam. "*Ennada*, what do you want now, looking into the house like that?" she asked, a little irritated.

"Amma," there, someone was calling her '*amma*' again, "Amma, can you tell Jyotsnakka that I am not coming tomorrow?"

She felt like a post office, passing on messages to her daughter or her son-in-law. But she was curious nonetheless, so she said, "But Arumugam, you just took the week off for Dasara. Now what ails you and your family?"

"Amma, my daughter is pregnant and I need to take her to the doctor," he was saying.

Several remarks such as "but you have a houseful of women

who can take her to the doctor", or "why can't your good for nothing son-in-law take her in a rickshaw", came to her mind and wound their way to the tip of her tongue.

But she didn't say anything. Because Arumugam was saying, "Amma, can you give me a loan of Rs 1000 for medical expenses? I will adjust it against my salary the coming month."

He was not giving her a choice, throwing all these requests to her from the window. She said, "Wait, let me call *chinamma* and see what she wants me to do."

Amma hesitated to call Jo though. Because, if Jo was in the middle of one of her high-powered budget meetings, she would be snappy.

She got up, just opened her Godrej almirah and gave Arumugam Rs 500, telling him to leave the window and put his mind into cutting the rose bushes. She prayed that her daughter wouldn't argue with her about giving money without consulting her first.

Why did grown-up children think that their parents' brains had diminished with age? After all, wasn't this the same parent who had brought them up, and quite successfully, she often wondered these days.

But Jo was a difficult girl. Even when she was young, she never saw reason. In truth, she had wanted to dial Jo's number, and in fact, she had done so, before hanging up abruptly and taking the decision to give the gardener money, just to get him out of her sight.

She didn't connect, as the young people said, with Jo anymore. Jo thought of her as an old person. She had just turned 65. That was not old, was it, she said to no one in particular.

The first thing Jo told her when they were building the house was that she had got a nice, big puja room for her.

But why did her daughter imagine she was going to spend long hours in the morning chanting *mantras*? Even when Jo's father, Nagaraj was alive, she had not felt the need to spend hours praying for her Nagu's health or her children's prosperity. Yet, they all did well for themselves, didn't they? True, Nagu had passed away a little too young and there were all those promises he had not kept.

He had promised to take her to Venice when he retired. But that was alright. She could always take the group tour for vegetarians that they were organizing these days. At least, now she didn't have to wake up in the morning to get him his filter coffee, so that he could go for his long walks on the beach. Yes, while he grew fit, she began to put on weight making nutritious meals for them. And she always made sure there was *dosa mavu* in the fridge so that her husband or the children never went hungry. Not a single day. Not even once.

No wonder she had morphed into the mother that one read about in children's stories, who was another metaphor for kindness and self-sacrifice. Or those Hindi movie mothers, who worked as maids somewhere, so that a young Amitabh could go to school (and later marry the glamorous Hema Malini).

She had had enough of being that iconic mother. Actually, any kind of mother. To top it all, her children now expected her to play the role of the good grandmother. They were urging her not to watch so much of television, but read stories of the *Ramayana* to their children. To teach them *sloka*s and tell them stories from the *Purana*s. They felt the children were reading too much of Harry Potter, which she didn't think was really all that bad. They thought their children were spending way too much time on the Net and on Facebook.

How was she to tell them she had asked her granddaughter Rasika to make her a 'member' of Facebook, and she was now making new friends, since her old school friends seemed to have died, or were too busy reading the *Purana*s and she couldn't find them on

Facebook? If only she didn't need Rasika's help to log on to the site, she too would have become an Internet addict, she thought to herself.

And yes, the way they imagined themselves to be such model youngsters made her want to speak of their childhood days. Jo, shall I tell Rasika how you flunked one class? Or you, Jan, how you took your guitar and ran away from home and stayed in Darjeeling smoking *hasish* with the hippies, until your father took the train from Madras to bring you back?

She wanted none of this. The kindness of her children in allowing her to stay with them, giving her a room. '*Paati*'s room', they fondly called it, where they expected her to hang family photographs of them as children and with their father. And fashioning a big *puja* room in each of their houses, in Madras and Bombay, imagining they would all go to hell if 'Amma' didn't propitiate the gods every morning.

Sometimes 'Amma' did think the gods had better things to do than to listen to the pleas and woes of human beings. That's why, even if she went to Tirupati with Nagu in an earlier time, she just stood and stared at Balaji, rather than ask him for a boon in the two seconds she had before him, before the impatient priests would shout, *jaragandi*, *jaragandi* in Telugu.

Jo sometimes spoke of taking her to Kashi. Fortunately, she didn't have enough leave. "Next year, Ma," she told her even as she was planning to pack her off to Jan's house in Bombay this coming summer, so that she and Rasika could go to Disneyland.

She didn't, as yet, have arthritis or cataract like her sister who lived in America with her daughter. Yet, every time she complained that her vision was somewhat blurred and she couldn't read the newspapers all that well, Jo would say, "Amma, I will take you to Shankara Netralaya. I am sure it's the cataracts." Or, when she complained a little leg pain, she said she would take her to an orthopaedic specialist.

No, she didn't want to go Shankara Netralaya or any other hospital in Madras. She wanted to go to the multiplex and watch a Brad Pitt film. And she didn't want to eat one more of those awful *ragi* biscuits and rusks that Jo bought for her, telling her they were good for her bones. Who said she couldn't have Oreo cookies?

She didn't want to be sitting in the house, minding the maids and gardeners. Or be cooking for the family. She wanted to go to the mall with Rasika and her friends, eat ice-cream and buy herself a pair of good Nike shoes. She wanted to get herself a membership in the gym. She wanted to remind the very modern Jo that Jane Fonda was about her age and wore leotards and exercised even after her marriage had gone bust.

She didn't want to go to Kashi either. She was quite certain of that. In fact, tomorrow she would call for a taxi and go to the travel agent to ask him how much it would cost to go to Venice. She would go there and lie in a gondola, having shaken off Jo and Jan and their constant 'concern' for her.

She saw that Raji was outside, knocking on the door for some advice, or for some recipe, no doubt. "Amma, how are you this afternoon?" Raji asked as she sat on the sofa next to her.

"Raji, I have a name," she said firmly.

"What, Amma, what are you saying? Did I offend you? You know I have always thought of you as my own mother, whom I miss very much."

"I have a name, Raji," she said softly. "My mother called me Mina, but in school and college they used to call me Meenakshi," she declared, getting up to look for her cell phone. She should be calling the travel agent really, and ask him to give her an itinerary for Venice.

LAST WORD

These days, I find a story in everything I see around me.

The purple lotus for instance that graces the cover. Who would think that in a country replete with lotuses in every pond and lake, it would be so difficult to find a lotus that would suit our needs? But indeed like the mythological Parijat, we have hunted for the lotus from the farthest reaches of Kashmir Valley to the deepest corners of Calicut. We finally found the healthy lotus at the right moment of bloom in the Sinha family pond in Tolouthu, Bihar! Nandini Murali clicked the photograph for us; And I thank Kamal Sahai who sent many young people across the country to look for the lotus.

A special thanks to Gitanjali Anand who designed the cover and the book with so much thought. Since we are family, she didn't even have the privilege of being able to throw designer's tantrums!

My friend, Sandhya Rao, to whom I first sent a bunch of stories asking, "do these sound like stories at all?" She not only thought they were worth publishing, but sat down to work on them. To Sandhya a big thank you for the first nod of approval.

Vinutha Mallya for encouraging me to publish with Mapin-Lit, when I had all but given up hope of seeing the stories in print.

Her notes in the margins made me sit up and rethink many of the things in the stories. Thanks are due to her and Neha Manke at Mapin Publishing for their editorial inputs.

To P Narendra of Pragati Printing who without any hesitation agreed to take up the book of stories, a small job for his famous press. Indeed, he would have been offended if I had gone elsewhere for printing 'The Purple Lotus...'.

What would acknowledgements be without a round of thank-you to all my friends? If you see yourselves in these stories, I admit some of your lives have been the triggers. But if you sound better in the stories, remember this is a work of fiction!

To my mother for reading every word I write. And to my father who was finally proud of me, even if I didn't become a famous banker like him. My children for vindicating that there is something I can do right!

To Shekar for being my fan, forever and now.